DITCHED

Kaylie Kay

Dedication

---

*To all of the crew who, like me, have had their wings
clipped during the Covid-19 pandemic.*

*May you be back up in the skies where you belong soon,
or find fulfilment in your next adventure.*

Table of Content

Chapter One

What was that horrendous buzzing sound?

Julie Margot tried to ignore it as she revelled in the fluttering kisses that Pablo was bestowing on her. She leaned back in her sun-lounger, listening to the rhythmic sounds of the Caribbean Sea and sipping her lychee daiquiri with extra rum, looking down at his tanned, glistening body as he ....

Something tickled her nose, and she brushed it away.

'Shall we swim, naked?' He looked up at her with a flash of white teeth and eyes as green as the ocean...

'Ooh yes,' Julie said, 'what a marvellous idea!' She jumped up and quickly removed her swimsuit. The beach was deserted, so no one would see. *Where was everyone, anyway?* she thought, confused.

The buzzing was getting louder, and whatever it was that had tickled her nose kept coming back, but she couldn't see it. Pablo was already in the water calling to her, but she felt disorientated, her surroundings were beginning to blur. She tried to see what it was but when she rubbed her eyes everything was getting dark.

Where was she?

Opening her eyes again she found herself in darkness with just a soft white light coming from behind her head, dimly lighting the padded walls that hemmed her in on all sides. There, just above her was something hanging, a string tickling her nose.

Was it night time? Was she at home?

Julie touched the object, making it swing away from her; it was something unfamiliar to her, and yet she had been here, in this tiny bed, before...

'Grab your mask and put it on, breathe normally.' A man with an Italian accent was telling her to put a mask on, but she was sure Pablo was Spanish, so it wasn't him... Julie was suddenly awake, catapulted out of her dream about Pablo and the Caribbean, and back into her crew bunk. She could hear muffled voices, and a shriek from the bunk next to hers. She grabbed at her oxygen mask and held it over her nose and mouth, eyes now opened wide to the darkness. Her ears popped as the plane began to descend at an alarming rate.

Antonio, the Italian purser, with his smooth Italian accent, sounded calm and reassuring. She could hear voices in the background as he spoke, passengers in the cabin clearly panicking. The fluttering in her stomach was threatening her own composure, and she focussed on her training, thirty years of drills that were embedded in her brain, hopefully never to be used.

Decompression when in crew rest

Seat Belt signs will illuminate

The white light from behind her

Continuous buzzer and masks drop out

Yes, that happened exactly as they said it would.

Don your mask and wait until the aircraft levels off

Donned! Waiting!

Make reassurance PA when possible

Well done, Antonio.

When safe to do so transfer to portable oxygen if necessary and return to cabin

She lay still and waited for that bit, planning how she would be the quickest one out of bed and down the stairs. What was next?

Check toilets for incapacitated passengers

She'd leave that to her crew, they all knew the same drills, but she was the manager, what did she have to do? Julie scrunched her eyes together, trying to picture the next part of the drill that lay deep inside the thousand-page manual which she thought she knew inside out.

If no word from the pilots, go to flight deck

Yes, that was it, she would go straight to the flight deck and they would tell her what the heck had happened, and what they were going to do about it. She tried to work out where they were, having left Seattle some hours ago. Over Canada? Over the Atlantic?

Julie felt the panic start to build; her usual calmness and 'everything will be fine' attitude might not actually work today. What if it was really bad and they had to make an emergency landing? She was lying in a bed inside a metal box up in the tail of their aircraft with four other crew. Would they all be found like this, still strapped to their bunks like they were in their coffins, her hairnet still on? She reached behind her and pulled it off – there was no way the rescue services were seeing her like some little old lady, dead or alive! All those handsome young men.

She threw her duvet back as her temperature rose, inwardly cursing her body for choosing now to have a menopausal flush, the first she had had in weeks. The next

4

problem hit her with the force of a jumbo jet and she stifled a cry as she realised; she was in just her underwear, and it didn't even match! *Julie!* she chastised herself. Always so meticulous, you never knew when someone might see your underwear after all, but she had let herself go a little lately, the flow of dates and spontaneous hook-ups had definitely been dwindling this last year or so. She couldn't bear it, the idea that she would be found amongst the plane wreckage in a floral bra and spotted green knickers, even if they were Victoria's Secret! The thought of the posthumous humiliation was unbearable, and Julie's jumbled thoughts digressed to why she hadn't packed pyjamas for crew rest, or slept in her uniform just this once like the others did? Right now, a creased blouse would have been such a minor issue in comparison.

Still they descended, Julie feeling the weightlessness of her body against the seatbelt that held her on her bed, wondering whether she would actually float to the ceiling that sat just a couple of feet above her if she undid it. She fought with the forces to sit up and reached to the bottom of her bunk, picking up her neatly folded uniform and struggling to put it on as the plane hurtled downwards. Crash or no crash, she would not be found like this!

****

Finally, they seemed to level out, and the captain's voice came over the PA.

'Sorry about that, ladies and gentlemen.' He sounded quite calm, she thought with relief. 'Well you may have gathered that we lost pressurisation there, due to reasons unknown at the moment, and had to descend rather quickly to a safe altitude. Rest assured though, we are now cruising at 10,000 feet and it is safe to breathe without your oxygen masks.' *Phew,* thought Julie, pushing hers to the side and checking with her fingers that her French twist hairstyle had survived.

'Unfortunately,' the captain continued, 'we are going to need to divert, and we are just speaking to people on the ground to find out our options. As soon as we know anything more we will be sure to let you know. Meanwhile please remain seated with your seatbelts fastened and follow the cabin crew's instructions. Cabin crew, you can move around the cabin, please prepare for landing.'

Seatbelts clicked open as the crew released themselves. Julie was out in a heartbeat, shuffling at speed to the foot of her bed and swinging her legs into the stairwell, descending through the door at the bottom that opened into the cabin. The galley below was a mess with debris everywhere. Juice and water jugs lay amongst hundreds of plastic glasses, and a metal atlas box was open on the floor, spilling its tea and coffee supplies everywhere. Julie's manager head noted that it had clearly not been latched into its stowage as it should have been, but she was discerning enough to know that now was not the time to be reprimanding crew, despite the fact that someone could have been injured.

'Is everyone okay?' she asked Antonio, who was kneeling down mopping up the floor with paper towels, beads of sweat running down the side of his face as he worked quickly.

'Yes, they are just out checking on the passengers now,' he affirmed without looking up.

Julie stepped over to the door and glanced out of the window. She was hugely relieved to see that they were over land, and not the ocean. Despite the pages of the manual that told them how to evacuate a plane on water, and the training the pilots had to land on it, she seriously doubted how successful they would be on the North Atlantic. Hopefully there was an airfield nearby which they could divert to quickly, she thought, as her legs were feeling decidedly shaky.

'Okay, I'll make a conference call once I've spoken to the boys,' she said as she walked into the aisle.

'Yes, boss,' Antonio replied.

Julie smiled at this and walked away. No one else ever called her 'boss' and she wasn't sure how she felt about it, but somehow in his Italian accent and from his sweet young face with those thick long eyelashes, it didn't bother her, or perhaps it was simply that she had much bigger things to worry about right now than the way her crew addressed her.

There was an unexpected calmness in the cabin as she walked towards the front. People were speaking in hushed voices to each other – she couldn't hear what they were saying, but she saw the way they looked up at her, studying her face for the reassurance which she was struggling to show. This wasn't turbulence, when she could sit opposite a terrified passenger and smile, tell them it was perfectly normal, because it wasn't. She tried to read their minds from their facial expressions, wondering how different their thoughts about the situation must be. Some would still be fearing death no doubt, whilst the optimists would be celebrating that the panic was apparently over; she wondered if anyone else had considered their choice of underwear?

As she passed the next galley there was a sudden, dull *thud*. It wasn't loud, but it seemed to shake the whole aircraft. In all her thirty years of flying Julie had never heard a noise like it and her stomach lurched. The interim calmness was replaced with gasps and cries. Her own heart started beating hard and fast in her chest as she sped up, her mind racing, trying to work out what on earth was going on now. She pressed forward through the cabin, her senses heightened, listening for clues as to what was happening to them. Behind the sound of the passengers she wondered if she was mistaken in thinking that the aircraft had fallen silent. The background noise of the engines, which was always there but you didn't notice because it was ever present, had been replaced by an eerie quietness. The half-smile that she had fixed on her face for the benefit of the passengers was gone now; even the most professional flight attendant couldn't pretend that things were okay anymore.

Chapter Two

Ditching

Julie's hands trembled, her palms sweating as she tapped the entry code into the small keypad next to the flight deck door and waited for the light to go green. She could hear the alarms ringing from outside, but as she pulled the door open they seemed to scream at her, telling her that things were *really* bad.

The two pilots sat hunched over their controls. Iain, the captain, was sitting on the left pressing buttons and cancelling the noises that were so distracting, a manual open on his lap. Warning signs flashed on the screens and buttons flashed red across the controls all around them. Through the windows Julie could see that the ground beneath them was far too close, the clouds that she usually looked down upon were way above them now. Julie perched on the edge of the jump seat behind them as she felt her legs go weak.

'Mayday, mayday, mayday. Osprey 454. We've suffered multiple bird-strike while making an emergency descent due to decompression in the cabin. Double engine failure, unable to relight so far.'

The first officer's words seemed to be coming from somewhere distant and Julie shook her head, forcing herself to stay in the spine-chilling moment. This was her job, this was why she suffered three days of training *every* year and refreshed her crew's knowledge in *every* briefing, just in case something like this ever happened, and seemingly it just had. As if a decompression hadn't been bad enough, now it appeared that they had flown straight into a flock of birds and lost both engines – someone higher up definitely had it in for them today.

'Continuing to attempt relight but anticipate emergency landing. Currently at 9,500 feet and descending.' Derren, the first officer who had been so jovial when they had checked out of the hotel earlier that day, turned a very worried face to Julie as he waited for a response on the radio.

'Prepare the cabin for an emergency landing, Julie, in case we can't relight these engines,' he said gravely.

The captain raised his hand sharply to stop them, without turning around. A finger from his other hand was poked purposefully on a spot on the map that was now unfolded in front of him.

'Prepare for ditching, if we can't get an engine relit, we will be landing in North Hudson Bay in less than nine minutes. Presume all exits useable, Julie, can you please make the PA to the passengers.' Julie looked out to the rugged terrain beneath them. For whatever reason, the captain was happier to take his chances landing on water than down there, and Julie had to trust his judgement. As she stood up she recalled the story of the captain who had landed his plane safely on the Hudson River just a few years back. Julie clutched at the glimmer of hope that it gave her, knowing that she would need it to get her through the next nine minutes.

Repeat back the briefing

Julie dragged her **Emergency landing on water drill** out from her now chaotic mind.

'Osprey 454,' the radio crackled and Derren turned back to attend to it. They both had their backs to her again now, no time to talk it through or reassure her that they would be okay.

'Prepare for ditching in eight minutes,' she acknowledged quietly, looking at her watch and heading out of the flight deck. Taking the deepest breath she had ever taken and filling her lungs, Julie picked up the handset by the nearest door and started her announcement. She so wished that she had time to brief her crew first, that they didn't have to find out like this along with the passengers, but there just wasn't.

'Ladies and gentlemen, well as if a decompression wasn't enough, unfortunately now we have suffered a severe bird strike resulting in a total engine failure.' Julie could hear the wobble in her usually so polished voice as she struggled to find the words to explain the disaster that was unfolding. It all felt so unreal, as if she was watching a training video based on something that had happened at another airline, and her mind drifted for a moment. She imagined classrooms of crew watching this and trying to identify the mistakes that were made which would result in the death of everyone on board... as if she wasn't in enough trouble at work as it was! Julie shook the thought off as it started to gather pace, forcing herself to concentrate on the reality; this story hadn't been finished yet, she thought defiantly. 'The flight deck are doing all they can to relight them, however just in case they aren't successful, we must prepare for an emergency landing on water...' She looked across at the two crew in the galley, the colour draining from their faces.

'Cabin crew, please prepare the galleys and cabin for ditching in approximately,' she glanced at her watch, time was disappearing too quickly, 'seven minutes.'

Julie nodded at the girls, giving them a focus, something to do. She was grateful for how their training was so embedded that they could go into autopilot, even though the last time they were in this situation it was in a pretend aircraft inside of a hangar at Heathrow Airport. For the passengers she knew that this would be the longest seven minutes of their lives.

'Passengers, please put on your life jackets now, *do not* inflate them until you are outside of the aircraft. You will find your life jacket underneath your seat.' She looked down the aisle and saw her crew busy helping people, showing them how to put their life jackets on, and felt so proud of these young boys and girls that she was overwhelmed for a moment and had to compose herself, again.

'At this time if we have any airline staff, firefighters, police, paramedics…' *basically any handsome man in uniform*, her mind wandered even at a time like this, 'who are willing to help, please make yourself known to a member of crew.' She watched as her crew followed her prompt and moved the most able of the passengers to the door areas, and wondered if they knew that they were volunteering to help evacuate the plane, or indeed do it alone should the crew member not be able to. She looked at her watch again; five minutes left. She was sure there was more to say, but without digging out her PA book from her bag she just couldn't remember. 'Now stay calm and have a look at where your nearest exits are, and practise your brace position.' She felt an urge to finish with something meaningful like 'God be with us all,' but she stopped herself, suspecting that it might not actually be very reassuring; anyway, she wasn't even religious, although perhaps right now was a good time to reconsider that.

Okay, Julie, think. What else did she need to do? She took her pen from where it was tucked into the waistband of her skirt and shakily wrote 134 + 11 on her hand, the total number of passengers and crew on board. She quickly stowed away her paperwork and handbag that had been at the side of her jump seat and cast her eye over the galley to make sure everything was secure. If she was going to die it wouldn't be because she hadn't latched a cart and it had flown out at her on impact, she thought, flashing back to the atlas box on the back-galley floor, back when they only had a decompression to worry about.

She sank down heavily into her seat and put her head in her hands, grateful that there was a wall between her and the front row of First Class, that they couldn't see her lose her composure for this brief moment. She felt the jump seat next to her move as Jody joined her.

'I've briefed the first two passengers on what to do if we aren't okay,' she said. Julie looked up and gave her a weak smile.

'Cabin crew, emergency stations,' the captain's voice cut through the heavy air that hung around them. Julie wished she hadn't looked out of the window, seeing the water getting closer by the second.

'Here,' Jody had grabbed their life jackets from underneath their seats and was prodding Julie with hers.

'Oh my goodness.' Julie had completely forgotten about the most important thing. 'Thank you, love,' she said, taking it from her and putting it on quickly, being careful not to catch her hair, before fastening her harness over the top. She reached down and took Jody's hand, giving it a squeeze and turning to look at her. Jody was leaning forward, her blonde hair pulled into the 'doughnut' style bun favoured by most of the girls, and then loosened to make it look less perfect. Her long fringe that she wore parted in the middle, fell in front of her face, but not before Julie had seen the tears running down it. Julie had flown with Jody many times before and had always loved this girl for her positive energy, and it made her so sad to see her cry. 'It will all be okay, Jody, this is what we are trained to do,' she said kindly. 'You'll get home to your little boy, don't you worry.'

Julie knew that Jody Green was a mum, and she couldn't begin to imagine how much worse this was for her. After all, if Julie died who would really care? She didn't have parents, or children, life hadn't taken her down that path. She had friends, but they weren't close ones, that being how she had chosen to live for reasons known only to her. She lived her life in the moment, happy to socialise at work and enjoy what London had to offer when she was home, but she couldn't think of anyone that would actually *miss* her. So, if this was how it ended, so be it, but for the sake of every other soul on board she hoped that it wasn't.

'Brace yourselves,' the captain commanded, and she did, sat on her hands, head pushed hard into her headrest, her eyes tightly shut.

'Heads down, feet back,' she shouted in unison with the other crew, over and over as they did in the rigs. She could hear Antonio bellowing from the back, and one of the girls screaming it out, whilst the rest of them provided the backing vocals to this soundtrack of impending doom. Everyone else was silent, even the plane, and through the open door behind her she could hear the warnings as a robotic voice counted down the last few hundred feet and warned the pilots to pull up.

The 'impact' was so subtle she might have missed it if she hadn't heard the computer announce that they were at zero feet. She reminded herself to breathe, still shouting her commands and reluctantly opened her eyes to confirm that they had actually landed. Spray was hitting the window in jets, and they seemed to go up and down over the water, as if on a boat powered by an engine. Only it wasn't a boat, it was a plane, and it was the lack of engines that had got them here, Julie thought hopelessly. She shut her eyes again, hoping again that it was all just a very bad dream...

As they slowed down Julie forced herself to look out of the window. She could see in the distance the shoreline of the lake or whatever this water was that they had landed on, and she wondered how far it really was away, if she could swim it...

'Julie.' Jody was nudging her, as a piercing horn started screeching next to her ear.

'This is an emergency, evacuate, evacuate,' Iain called out over the PA as they came to some sort of halt, although it was hard to judge with the movement of the water outside.

Julie threw off her harness and jumped up, relying on muscle memory to carry her through as inside she felt paralysed with fear. She pressed the white illuminated button that switched off the horn, before looking out of the window to check that the water was below the door. In the training rig there was never anything outside the window, you just had to pretend, and so the presence of real water was utterly terrifying. Still Julie's body continued to follow the drills... A quick pull of the handle and the door flew open under its own power. With a *whoosh* the huge grey rubber slide-raft unfolded, instantly inflating on the water in front of her, exactly as it was supposed to do. Julie smiled despite herself, marvelling for a moment at how things were going just as they had said they would go in training; perhaps things were going to look up now, she thought with a surge of optimism.

'Okay, it's ready,' she announced with some pride, standing back against the wall and holding on to the assistance handle next to her.

'Open your seatbelts, come this way,' Jody bellowed next to her, reminding Julie of the actual commands that she should be shouting, and the less casual tone that she should be using.

'Yes, open your seatbelts and come this way!' Julie called, not as loudly as Jody; she couldn't bring herself to be so crass, much to the annoyance of her safety trainers year after year. As passengers ran towards them Julie looked back out of the door, marvelling at the fact that they were floating so well.

'Follow me!' Jody's cry was unexpected, and snapped Julie back into the present. She watched open-mouthed as her crew member went against all protocol and jumped first into the raft, calling people towards her as she seated herself firmly next to the strap that would separate it from the aircraft. Julie resisted the urge to follow her, staying put where she was to lead the evacuation. She totally understood the poor girl's desperation but she was the manager, and *she* had to follow procedures!

'Crawl to the ends, sit either side,' she repeated politely as they passed her. 'I'll take that, sir,' she said, deftly removing a cabin bag from a suited businessman as he tried to exit with it. He tried to pull it back, but Julie fixed him with the stare that she had perfected over the years, pushing him in the small of his back firmly towards the raft as he loosened his grip.

'Ooh be careful,' she said to the young girl carrying a baby who was swamped by the infant life jacket it was wearing.

They passed in a blur – never in all her years of flying had Julie seen people get off an aircraft so quickly, and the cabin was soon empty. Julie reached into the safety equipment cupboard next to the door and started throwing its contents into the raft, the things she mindlessly checked before every flight but never took out:

Medical kit

Loudhailer

Radio beacon

Water pouches

Defibrillator

Makeup bag…

Still they floated, and Julie got braver, venturing into the cabin to see if there was anyone left behind, grabbing armfuls of blankets on her way.

'Julie, we need to get off,' the captain was calling her and she turned to see him beckoning impatiently from the door.

'Coming,' she called calmly. She felt strangely secure and confident, everything seemed so normal inside the aircraft. It was as if everyone had just got off at an airport somewhere and she was doing a quick check of the cabin.

'Hurry up, woman, for God's sake,' he shouted impatiently.

'I said I'm coming,' she retorted indignantly, stomping back up the cabin in protest. They might have spent the night together once many years ago, but it certainly didn't mean he could talk to her like *that*! She couldn't help noticing that he was wearing his hat and she rolled her eyes. Some of them were so full of their own importance, they were about to try to stay afloat in a rubber raft on an enormous lake in the middle of nowhere but he clearly still needed everyone to know he was the captain, she thought with disdain.

Reaching the door, she stopped for one last second and looked down at the raft and its passengers. Jody sat with her hand ready to pull the separation strap and two rows of faces stared back at her with expressions ranging from terror to delirium, all silent.

'Sorry, ladies and gentlemen, I was just getting a few essentials,' she apologised, throwing in the blankets and reluctantly taking Iain's hand to steady herself. Julie squeezed in next to Jody and pushed her back up against the side of the raft, her legs stretched out in front of her. She noticed a mark on her shoe and leaned forward to rub it off, thinking that even at a time like this it wouldn't do to drop one's standards. Sitting back again she could feel the water ripple underneath them, finding something strangely calming in its motions.

Jody pulled the strap sharply and they slowly began to drift backwards, away from the aircraft. As the distance between them got further Julie marvelled at how majestic the floating plane looked. The sun reflected off its polished fuselage, its tail pointing skyward, wings spread out like a fallen bird... until it suddenly sank in a matter of seconds.

Julie gulped. Perhaps her sense of security when she was still onboard was very ill judged after all, perhaps she should have hurried a little more.

Chapter Three

_____

30 years earlier

Julie sat upright, her shoulders back, ankles crossed and knees together, just like she had read in an article about interview skills. She looked around the circle of chairs in the room, at all of the other hopefuls, wondering if any of them were fighting the voices in their heads like she was.

They'll never want you, why would they? You're just plain little Julie Shuttleworth, not even your own parents wanted you so why would they?

'Julie?'

Julie looked up at the beautiful air hostess who sat behind the table at the front of the room with her male counterpart. She was everything that Julie wanted to be, a picture of glamour with her immaculate hair and red lipstick, a kind smile on her face that made Julie smile back and silenced her demons.

'Oh, I'm sorry,' Julie apologised, hoping that her momentary absence hadn't just cost her the job.

'That's okay, if you could just tell us a little about yourself.'

That's right, tell them, tell them all, they mocked. *Tell them about your mum! Tell them that you got caught stealing food at ten years old and taken into care. Tell them how no family ever wanted to adopt you! Tell them that you failed all your exams and that you lied on your application. Tell them….*

Julie felt the heat rising up her neck as everyone looked at her. She hated them, the voices that were always there, echoing all of the things people had said to her time and time again, telling her that she wasn't good enough. Well she *was* good enough! She was here because she finally believed that, because the bullies had gone now and the grown-up world had been kinder to her than the childhood one.

'Hi.' She fixed a smile on her face, the one she had practised in the mirror all week. 'I'm Julie, I'm twenty-two years old and it has always been my dream to fly.' She looked at the interviewers, who were smiling broadly back at her, spurring her on. 'I grew up in Surrey with my parents and two sisters.'

Lies, they hissed.

'Dad was a pilot and mum used to be crew, so we travelled a lot with them, and it was all I ever wanted to do.' She kept talking, not stopping for long enough for them to speak again, or for her to hear them. 'I finished school with 8 GCEs and then went to college to do Hair and Beauty. For the past four years I've been working in a department store, building up my customer service experience in order to be able to apply for this job.'

GCEs? You?! They mocked. *More like a degree in dropping out! College?! How hilarious, all you know about beauty is from the Avon magazine!* They were howling with spiteful laughter, but Julie didn't care, no one else could hear them, and the interviewers were nodding positively at her. At no point in her application had they asked for any proof of her exam results, and she *had* worked at a department store, since they too had believed the falsehoods on her application form and blindly hired her.

'Well it certainly sounds like you have a great background for the job, Julie,' the lady interviewer said, her partner nodding his head in approval.

Julie smiled and looked around her, absorbing the looks of admiration and perhaps envy at her charmed upbringing from around the room. She had told that story so many times now that she almost believed it herself, and she loved nothing more than to remember those great family holidays she had conjured up. They were just memories after all, a series of pictures stored in the mind, whether they were real or not. Julie could have had any upbringing she wanted, and that was the one that she had chosen.

****

The post hit the mat in the hall and Julie jumped up as quickly as she had done every morning this week. She was grateful to be working the late shift, so that she could be here when her letter finally arrived, and today was the day that it did, by the looks of the big brown envelope on the floor.

Dear Julie,

We are delighted to offer you….

Her hands shook, the rest of the letter blurring as she tried to read it, she had got the job, she *was* good enough! The voices were silent, there was nothing that they could say. None of it mattered, what had happened before today was all history, and now she had the future she had dreamed of in her hands. Julie Shuttleworth was going to be an international air hostess! She was going to walk through the airports of the world pulling a little black case behind her, with her head held high. People were going to turn to look at her, so glamorous she would be. She was going to drink cocktails on Caribbean beaches, shop in New York City, party in Hong Kong… and the best thing of all was that the memories she would make now would all be real.

She sat on the armchair and looked around her small living room, and smiled. She could have let them beat her, the voices; she could have believed what they said. But despite everything, she had made it. She had seen some of the girls from the children's home turn to prostitution and drugs, but Julie was stronger than that, life had made her that way. Her home might not have been much to some people, but the flat which her social worker had found her was nicely furnished, with thick velvet curtains and matching soft furnishings. That was why she had picked the department store as her first job, for the discounts, so that she could make herself the nice home that she had always wanted. Everything that Julie did had a purpose, it was what kept her focussed, kept her sane. She had been good at her job too, her managers told her that she was. She had made some friends, maybe not like the ones normal young girls had, the childhood ones you told everything, but friends nonetheless, who invited her out for drinks, and didn't pry too much into her past. Now she was going to go and tell them all that she was leaving, and she knew they would be happy for her, that they all knew it was her dream job.

Putting her coat on, Julie glanced at the phone on the table. In her imaginary life she would have picked up the handset from its cradle and called her parents, and her sisters. She smiled as she imagined how happy they would be for her, how proud Mum and Dad would be that she was following in their footsteps, playing the conversations in her head as she walked to the bus stop. Such highs always had to have a low though, she had learned from a young age, and it soon came. She allowed herself to think for a second about her real parents, something that she deliberately didn't do often. Maybe Dad really was a pilot? Mum didn't know what he did, at least that was what she had said, just a meaningless one-night stand when she had drunk too much was all she had ever managed to get out of her. Mum had never been an air hostess though, that was for sure.

You'll never get through the training, you're not good enough!

And that was why she didn't allow the thoughts in, or the *real* memories. Nothing, and she meant *nothing*, about her childhood brought her any happiness, just darkness and misery. She slammed the box that held the real memories shut, but not quickly enough. One picture was left, and it was always the same one. There was mum, on the floor, her eyes open...dead.

Julie could see herself, just ten years old, standing frozen to the spot. She felt the mix of emotions as if she was right back there... the intense sadness that her mum was gone, to enormous relief. Relief that the woman who had neglected her, left her to fend for herself while she lost herself in bottles of gin and vodka every night, never getting up to see her off to school, never helping her with her homework, never telling her she loved her, wasn't able to make her feel bad anymore... No more shouting, no more being told she was useless, no more drunken rages and hurtful insults... But then had come the overwhelming guilt, that she had never been able to make her happy, that she had caused her own mum so much unhappiness that she had actually killed herself...

For days Julie had carried on as normal, going to school each day, while mum lay under a blanket, too heavy for her to move. She didn't know who to tell, or what to do, and there was no one she could turn too, her and mum had no friends. Then the electric had run out, and she had no more coins to put in the meter, and finally the food. That was when she was caught stealing, and the kind policewoman who had finally asked her what was going on and listened to her story had cried when she told her. It was the first kindness Julie could remember, and she had felt hopeful that life was going to get better for her then, but it didn't...

'Where to, love?' The bus driver interrupted her and Julie looked at him blankly through the wall of tears that had filled her eyes. She didn't recall the bus arriving, let alone getting onto it. Julie picked up that last picture of her mum, the worst of her *real* memories, from her mind's floor and threw it in the box with the others. This time she locked it, and threw the key as far away as she could, she would never go in there again.

'Oxford Street, please.'

Chapter Four

Ditching + 00:10hrs

Julie's eyes were fixed to the spot where the plane had been just moments ago, her mind frozen in shocked realisation of how close she had been to sinking with it. They sat in silence for some time, until eventually the captain's voice broke it, booming through a loudhailer.

'Well, ladies and gentlemen, if I can have your attention please,' he was addressing all of the rafts that floated around them. 'Please stay calm, the worst is definitely behind us now and we are extremely pleased to have been able to land and get you all off the aircraft safely against all the odds,' he said with self-indulgent pride. 'We will have you to shore shortly and the emergency services will soon be here to get you all home. We, your crew, are highly trained for these situations so rest assured you are in safe hands.' He put the loudhailer down. 'And you, ladies and gentlemen,' he addressed those in their raft, 'are in especially good hands with myself, please call me Iain, or Captain if you prefer, and Derren your first officer here.' He signalled to the so far mute first officer who raised his hand and managed a small smile. Julie liked Derren, he had a young family if she remembered rightly, and an uninflated ego, unlike some. 'Julie,' Iain said, bending down and talking much quieter, 'where we will find the paddles?'

Julie blinked; she had been poised to accept her own introduction and gratitude, but clearly she wasn't getting any, she realised, somewhat offended.

Well no point sulking, Slide Raft Equipment, she thought, picturing the manual pages she needed.

Canopy – in the bag at the end, hopefully they wouldn't need it though as land didn't seem that far away.

Leak stoppers, signalling mirror, flares, sponge, water purification tablets, bailing bucket, all in the survival kit attached to the side. Should she suggest using the **sea dye**? Or the **anchor**? Probably not, she decided, it didn't seem like they were going to be in the water for too long, the land was definitely getting closer.

She looked over the side to see if the rope for survivors to hold on to and the rope ladder were there like they should be – they were. Now if only they were floating off Barbados, this was a catamaran and they were all jumping in for a nice swim between cocktails, it wouldn't be so bad, she thought, digressing.

Now paddles, where were they?

'We don't have them anymore, remember?' Jody interrupted. 'They took them off a few years back.'

'Oh yes, so they did,' Iain said unconvincingly, and Julie could tell that he had no idea about the contents of the raft, that the safety training beyond landing the plane was something he considered was not his concern. How irritating, then, that he should still want to be taking the credit for everything, she thought. She couldn't help noticing how he had positioned himself at the front left of the raft too, just as he sat on the plane, just in case anyone should still be confused about his position as captain. 'Well the current seems to be pulling us to shore anyway, so not to worry,' he said to no one in particular.

'Captain, we are heading for shore,' Antonio was calling them from where he sat at the helm of his own ship. Julie looked around at the eight little boats that were floating so bizarrely on the water, each headed by a crew member in an orange life jacket, while their passengers wore yellow. *They* all got to be in charge, to be their ship's captain and everybody's hero, but not the actual flight manager, noooo, she was outranked by *the twat in the hat*. Julie raged, hating that she herself had once fuelled his overinflated ego by sleeping with him.

'Thank you, captain, for saving our lives,' the businessman who she had wrestled the bag from began to clap at her side, followed by the other passengers in their raft. Despite everything, Julie couldn't deny that he had shown some skill in landing the plane on water, and in dealing with not one, but the two emergencies that had got them here. She clapped her hands together softly; she was reluctantly grateful too. Iain visibly inflated, his chest puffing out like a proud bird on a wildlife documentary.

'And to the ladies that got us out too, well done, girls.' The elderly man who sat still holding his wife's hand smiled and nodded at her and Jody.

'Thank you,' Julie said gratefully, suspecting that he had noticed her own need for recognition, old people were always so wise and in tune she found.

'Yes, yes, well done, girls,' Iain concurred, clapping his hands with about as much vigour as she had used for him.

Julie looked around the raft, for the first time really seeing the people who she was sharing it with. The businessman, mid-forties with thick dark hair and clean shaven, was sitting next to her. He had taken off his jacket in the warm sun, and removed his tie, and was looking down at his lap. She didn't know what to make of him yet, still a little annoyed that he had tried to take his bag off with him, and so she was reserving her judgement. Next the old couple, who were sitting with such serene expressions on their faces that Julie immediately felt calmer just from looking at them. Still holding hands; she wondered if they were even able to let go of each other, or if they were actually bonded with glue or something, and she laughed inside at the thought.

Ditched

Then a young couple with a baby, perhaps in their late twenties. The baby was cocooned in a yellow infant life jacket with an inflated ring around it that was making it quite impossible for the parents to hold it close, and the mother had taken to bouncing it up and down. Despite them smiling and cooing at their child she could see the fear in their eyes, recognising their intense sense of responsibility to protect their offspring, something she couldn't really relate to but thought she understood nonetheless.

On the other side of the raft a young girl of perhaps six or seven with shiny golden hair and wearing flowery pink leggings was holding her mother tightly. The mother was mid-thirties, with shoulder-length highlighted hair and an understated elegance, and she smiled back at Julie. To her left a couple of about Julie's age, she remembered them from seat 1A and 2A. *She* had been utterly obnoxious at the start of the flight, all designer wear and no manners, whilst he had been an outrageous flirt. On another day she would have given them very little thought, but she looked forward to finding out more about them now that they were going to have this extra time together; there was usually a reason why a woman was in a bad mood, and more often than not it was because of a man, Julie knew this well.

And then there was Eyecandy! Julie laid her eyes on the surprise guest, all muscle-clad six foot two or more of him, how had she not noticed him as he had climbed out of her door? With thick, wavy blonde hair and a beautiful chiselled face he was far too young for her, but once upon a time he

33

would have been exactly her type. There was a day when she wouldn't have thought twice about the age gap, but she was having to admit lately that perhaps she had reached the top of her hill… and gone over it, that Julie Margot was no longer the irresistible blonde bombshell she had once been. The thought made her sad, like it always did.

He was looking down at his phone, smiling at it, probably telling his gorgeous girlfriend that he was safe, and how much he loved her. Well, girlfriend or no girlfriend, and far too young or not, he would brighten up the otherwise grim situation over the coming hours or, heaven forbid, days.

Lastly was the quiet man from First who had said nothing much to anyone since he had boarded. He was tired, he had said, politely declining drinks or food, and going straight to bed. People like him were the best customers, the ones who wanted nothing! Julie studied him. Probably about her age, dark hair, cropped short around the sides. Slim, which was admirable in men over fifty, and he looked 'nice.' That was the only word she could think of right now, she would dig a little deeper later.

So that made twelve passengers and four crew, sixteen souls on board, the other 129 spread between the remaining seven rafts. She was glad that they had a light load as otherwise they would have been much more cramped. You had to look hard for positives at a time like this, but it was something which Julie did particularly well, having spent a lifetime finding positives in bad situations.

Ditched

****

They all sat largely in silence as they drifted towards land. Everything was just so surreal, and it seemed to Julie that everyone had a whole lot of thought processing to do. She couldn't have verbalised her own feelings, so jumbled and unreadable they were, and so she focussed instead on the people she was here with. She smiled as she watched them all, presuming that each and every one of them was thanking some higher being for getting them out of the plane alive. She didn't look away when they would look up and catch her watching them, and slowly one by one they returned her smile and she felt their unspoken feelings cover the raft in a warm blanket. These complete strangers had just been bonded by an experience that no one else would ever have, and so nobody else would ever understand except each other.

'Julie, pleased to meet you.' She turned and offered her hand to the person on her left.

'Milton.' He took her hand and held it with both of his. So, the businessman had a name. Julie smiled at him and saw his face soften, a new person breaking through from behind the frozen face he had worn thus far.

'Nice to meet you, Milton, sorry about the circumstances.'

'Yes well, I'll look forward to filling out my survey when the airline sends it to me.' This made Julie laugh as she imagined the responses they would get from this flight.

Of course you would expect every one of her crew to be given a medal for evacuating the aircraft like they had, but there was bound to be at least one passenger that wouldn't see past the whole inconvenience of it all and mark them as 'poor' for not ensuring they were still offering a full drinks and meal service in the raft. She didn't think Milton would though, she could see a kindness in his eyes as he held her hand.

'I'm sorry if I seemed a little short when I took your bag off you.' Julie wasn't sure why she was apologising, but she felt that her earlier judgment of him had been somewhat harsh.

'Oh, not at all, I'm so embarrassed that I did that, I don't know what I was thinking.' He shook his head. 'I think I just wasn't thinking at all, I'm sorry I even tried to keep hold of it.'

Julie got it, he had just been acting on impulse, not thinking at all. What did you think about at a time like that after all, other than getting the hell off there? He hadn't had the benefit of training, drills to follow, like she had.

He had let go of her hands now, and appeared so much more relaxed as he sank back into the inflated wall of the raft. Julie leaned over him to the older gentleman, who already had his hand extended to receive hers. He was in his seventies, she guessed by the thick skin and lines on his face and his thinning grey hair, but he still looked strong and his eyes sparkled with an inner youth.

'My love, it's a pleasure to meet you,' he said, shaking her hand vigorously. 'This is my beautiful wife Bet, and I'm Eric.' His wife was beaming beside him. Julie guessed she was about the same age, but women had the gift of cosmetics and Bet had made use of all of them to defy the years, along with her bleached blond hair. She noticed how they both had deep smile lines etched down either side of their faces from the outer corners of their eyes, and how lovely they were, telling a story of a life led with much happiness in it. In her world no one seemed to have lines anymore, but some weren't so bad after all.

'Well it's lovely to meet you both,' she replied, feeling her smile widen. 'Please accept my apologies for the current situation.'

'You saved our lives, dear gal, you have nothing to apologise for, and we have everything to thank you for,' he said, and now she noticed his London accent. He was fixing her with a serious look to make sure she understood him.

'Thank you,' Julie said, humbled by his gratitude. She looked up to see the others all looking over at them, each waiting for their own introductions, waiting to give their names and join in with the forming stage of this new team. Julie looked to the shore to see if they had time, deciding that they did. This was what she did every flight, formed a new team, and today it didn't matter that they weren't all crew, because right now every single one of them had a lead role in this disaster movie that she was starring in.

'Ladies and gentlemen, I'm Julie, your flight manager and this is Jody,' she introduced them to Jody who gave them a small wave and smile – she looked worried, Julie realised, and she instinctively knew why. 'If anyone has a mobile telephone on them that she could borrow just to call her son, I am sure she would be extremely grateful.'

Several hands went up, offering their phones to the young girl, who let a few small tears escape as she gratefully took the nearest one. Julie manoeuvred herself around to give her colleague some privacy, rolling her eyes when she caught sight of the captain behind them. He was standing like a ship's figurehead, hand across his brow and all, and was still clearly focussed on his own important role and leaving her to deal with 'the cabin'.

'Can I suggest we go around and introduce ourselves whilst we have this time before we land, I mean *get to land*.' Julie sniggered at her mistake before continuing with her restructured pre-flight briefing. 'And if you have any skills that may be of use… medical training and such like.' She was going to add camp-building, see if they had any grown-up scouts amongst them, but decided it was too early to suggest they might need overnight accommodation. Hopefully their rescue was already on its way. 'This is Milton,' she started them off. 'And Eric and Bet.' They each raised their hands in salutation. She looked to the next person, and gave them a nod to continue.

'Chloe,' said the girl who was still bouncing her inflatable baby, her luxuriously long and thick dark hair shimmering in the sunlight. 'And this is Luke.' She looked up to her partner with adoration, stroking his fashionable beard with her fingers. 'And *this* is Reuben.' Everyone looked at the little face as she turned him around, his tiny hands poking out either side of his life jacket. He beamed at them all, showing his gums, completely unaware of the gravity of their situation.

Bet was leaning over him now, a grandmotherly smile on her face. 'What a beauty he is too, looks a little bit like Ethan, don't you think, dear?' Eric nodded his agreement. 'Good sleeper?'

'Not usually,' Chloe answered, with a grimace. 'He likes to see what is going on.'

'I'm glad someone is enjoying his day out,' said Luke with a hint of irony, putting his arm around his partner and squeezing her affectionately. Julie looked and noticed that neither of them wore wedding rings, and thought it was a shame that a couple so clearly in love hadn't found the time or perhaps the money to get married yet, when so many much less suited couples managed to make it happen.

'Luke's a builder,' Chloe said proudly.

'Well that could come in very useful if we end up here for the night.' Milton voiced what she had been afraid to say. The ground around them was very rough, and they had to consider that rescue might take some time; if the grey clouds that she could see in the distance were coming in their direction, they could need some protection from the elements, especially the young and old amongst them. 'Ex scout by the way, and national den-building champion,' Milton added with a smirk, answering another of her previous unspoken thoughts. Was he reading her mind? she wondered, aware that her mind was a place that no one else should ever have access to, and telling herself not to be so silly, mind readers were just a myth, *weren't they*? She turned to the other side of the raft, and its next passengers, trying to keep her thoughts on track.

'Anna, and this is Ruby.' The lady spoke in an American accent, and stroked her daughter's hair out of her face as she talked. 'Ex flight attendant.'

'Oh, how lovely,' Julie said with enthusiasm. She would have had the same training for one thing, but most importantly she would be good with people and being an effective team member, it wasn't something that came naturally to everybody.

'Did you ever have a day as bad as this one when you were flying?' Eyecandy asked with a charming, lopsided grin.

'Heck no, the worst I ever had was moderate turbulence, and I thought I was going to die then. I don't think I was really cut out for it,' she laughed, making the others smile. Julie could feel that people were starting to lighten up, allowing themselves to relax a little. She would talk to her more later, but they were really close to the shore now and she still had four more people to get to.

'Phil, nice to meet you all, and this is my wife Cheryl.' It was the couple from 1A and 2A. He was still smiling broadly, flashing two rows of expensive dental veneers or implants that he was obviously very proud of. Cheryl didn't smile, barely looking up to receive her introduction. 'Plastic surgeon, not sure how useful that will be today but I have medical training of course.'

'Ooh, how interesting,' Julie cooed. She had been having Botox for years now of course, and occasional facial fillers, but recently she had noticed a definite loosening around her jowl line. In fact, everything had been getting looser lately, age had been trying to creep up on her in recent years. Perhaps she could secure herself a nice little discount on the back of saving his life, she pondered for a moment. 'Lucky you, Cheryl, lots of free treatments,' Julie said, trying to find a common ground to connect with her on.

'Yes, lucky me,' Cheryl said flatly. Phil shifted uncomfortably and smiled even wider as if to compensate for his wife's miserable persona. Julie felt the sting of rejection, knowing that any further attempts at making conversation would be rebutted, and she had enough on her plate without becoming a marriage guidance counsellor.

'Craig.' Eyecandy spoke, he had a confidence and manner that intrigued Julie, and she wondered where someone so young had developed such self-assurance.

'And what do you do, Craig?' she asked, never one to hold back when she had a burning question.

'I'm an actor,' he said, explaining everything.

'I knew I recognised you from somewhere, weren't you in... ' Chloe interrupted. She was leaning forward over her baby, her eyes wide. Julie listened to them discuss his film roles, reminding her of someone she had known once.

'That's us, folks.' Iain's voice cut off the excited conversation in the boat, and they watched as Derren jumped into the waist-deep water, leaving his trousers and shoes in a neat pile where he had just been sitting a minute before. 'We are just going to get us as close to the shore as possible so that you don't get too wet.'

Derren was pulling the mooring line, which had once attached them to the aircraft, over his shoulder and attempting to pull them to shore. She looked along as the other rafts made their own landings, seeing that they all had two or more people pulling theirs; it took her back for a second to her ditching training, when they all had to get in the pool fully clothed, swim a length to get their life jacket, put it on, and rescue each other into a raft in the middle. This situation bore absolutely no resemblance whatsoever!

'I think he may need a hand,' she suggested to Iain, who pretended not to hear her. 'Iain,' she raised her voice, 'I think he needs help.' She could tell that he had no intention of getting wet himself, that he was deliberately ignoring her. She knew enough about captains like him. Perhaps she could have jumped in herself, but she was still old-fashioned and liked men to be chivalrous.

Splash

The one person who she hadn't gotten around to introducing, the quiet man from First Class, had jumped into the water, leaving a similar pile of clothes to Derren's behind. It seemed that a second man had just stripped off right in front of her, and she had missed it both times! The pair were standing only ankle deep now as they played tug-of-war with the raft, and she couldn't help but notice her mystery passenger had a very strong looking pair of legs, in contrast to his pilot accomplice.

'Well done, gentlemen.' Iain's voice made her angry, his pathetic congratulations were insulting, she thought. A long time ago she had had respect for the four stripes on a captain's shoulders, but now it had to be earned, and this one was currently failing to gain any stripes from her.

Chapter Five

27 years earlier

'See you in New York,' Julie said, standing on the pointed toes of her work shoes to reach up and wrap her arms around his neck. It was the height of summer, and the sun was already rising despite the ungodly hour. She was sure she could sense the curtains in neighbouring windows twitching as she kissed him goodbye, and so she kissed him for longer. They needed to know that Julie Margot was here to stay, that she would be moving into this lovely big house in their upmarket part of town very shortly, and that as Paul's choice of girlfriend she was good enough to be one of them.

'I can't wait to move in next week,' she said excitedly as she reluctantly pulled away. He had officially asked her this morning in acknowledgement of it being their two-year anniversary. 'I love you, Paul.'

'I love you too, keep the bed warm,' he winked at her and she rolled her eyes. She would make sure that by the time his flight arrived a few hours after hers, he would have much more than a warm bed to greet him. She had been planning for a week, and would have just about enough time to get to all the shops she needed to and to prepare herself... he would be well rewarded for his commitment to her.

She pulled her crew bag behind her down the path, sashaying like a catwalk model just for his benefit as he stood watching from the doorway. Putting the bag in the passenger seat of the tiny red sports car that she had bought for herself after her training three years ago, she turned and blew him a kiss before climbing into the driver's side. If Julie was going to be the flight attendant she had dreamed of being then she was going to do it properly, starting with the car, and then on to the pilot husband. That part was one step closer now, and she was confident that it wouldn't be long if things continued to be as good as they were.

Julie drove to the airport with a smile on her face the whole way. Everything she did had a purpose, was planned, and it was all going exactly how she had ordered it. And the best thing was that she had found Paul, the sensitive, sweet, and devastatingly handsome pilot who adored her back; she was a lucky girl and she knew it. Her only concession had been that he wasn't a captain yet, but that would come soon enough, it was a rite of passage, and by the time she had his babies they would be living in an even bigger house, with a huge garden for their children to play in, there was no doubt in her mind.

Today was a great day…

****

'Julie!'

Julie snapped out of her daydreams to see Lisa from her training course smiling down at her. She jumped up from the sofa in the crew lounge to hug her old friend.

'Don't tell me you're on the New York?!' Julie asked – she hadn't seen Lisa for over two years as they lived so far apart from each other and had never been rostered a flight together.

'No, babe, I wish I was, Lagos for me,' she groaned, they both knew the challenges of those flights. 'I've got ten minutes though, when's your briefing?'

'Two hours ago, the plane was late in.' At this rate Paul would be getting to New York before her, in fact he would probably be arriving at check-in very soon, she realised when she looked at her watch – her plans were falling apart by the minute.

'Oh, that's a pain in the arse,' said Lisa.

'So, what have you been up to?' Julie asked. 'Any man in your life?'

'Nooooo,' Lisa laughed. 'You know me, babe, I'll think about settling down when I'm about fifty!'

Julie did know, she had spent six weeks renting a room in the same house as Lisa during their training, and she could remember each of the 'visitors' she'd had, a constant delivery of men who very rarely made a second appearance. Julie was by no means a prude, but she had never seen the point of one-night stands, how could they contribute anything to her life plan? No, she had even made Paul wait to get her into bed, she needed to make sure he was in it for more than just a quick shag in the flight deck crew rest like others before him had offered!

'Done him,' Lisa nodded towards a pilot who was signing in at the desk by the door. 'Small penis.'

Julie stifled a laugh as she looked at the nondescript middle-aged man. 'Did you have your beer goggles on?'

'Most definitely,' Lisa giggled. 'There's been a few that I can blame on the wine. How about you?'

'Settled down, gorgeous man, I couldn't be happier,' Julie gushed.

'Oh, babe, I'm so happy for you.' Lisa leaned forward and hugged her. It felt so good to have someone be happy for her that Julie felt her own happiness overflowing. Lisa was the first person that she had told who had genuinely cared, and she wished they had lived closer to each other as she felt they would possibly be *good* friends, the type of friends that she was still lacking. Perhaps she should put these on her plan, as that was the only way that things seemed to happen for her. 'Really I am, make sure I get a wedding invite. I'm gutted I have to go now, my briefing's just starting.' They both stood up and hugged again. 'Give me a call some time, stay in touch,' Lisa said.

'I will do, have a great flight.'

Lisa leaned forward and Julie presumed she was going to hug her again, but she was whispering in her ear.

'And there were some I didn't need my beer goggles on for, like this one, shame he's got a girlfriend or I might have applied for that job.'

Julie turned to see who she was talking about, surprised to see Paul walking casually by, oblivious to them both. Julie turned her head quickly one way and then the other, desperately looking for the man of whom Lisa spoke, but there was no one else there and a surge of nausea overcame her whole body. She stared desperately after Paul, *her* Paul, watching him until he disappeared into the pilot's briefing room.

'Hot, huh?' Lisa had obviously mistaken her look of horror for one of appreciation. 'Couple of months ago in Barbados, ten out of ten in the sack. Gotta go.'

And that was that, Lisa was gone and for the second time in her life the bottom had fallen out of Julie Shuttleworth's world.

****

'Is there anyone on the early New York that can go on the Los Angeles, one of their crew has just had to be stood down?' A manager was standing in the middle of the lounge area addressing the crew that were sitting around still waiting for the plane to New York to be cleaned. Julie shot up her hand. She had been numb, in a trance this past half an hour, and had just been contemplating faking a migraine and going home. She had an overwhelming urge to run away, and definitely not to New York where he would be. She needed more than a seven-hour flight to sort out how she felt, and more importantly, what she was going to do. The one thing she did know already though was that she wouldn't be confronting Paul, or jeopardising her future by letting something like infidelity ruin what she had.

'Thank you, have you got a suitcase?' he asked. Julie shook her head, she had only packed enough for one night in New York into her little black case. She had planned to buy the champagne and food for their anniversary picnic in Central Park when she arrived.

'Fantastic, what's your name and payroll?'

'Julie Shuttleworth 041356.'

He wrote it on a piece of paper. 'That's great, you can go straight to the plane, it's just boarding at Gate 102.'

'No problem, happy to help,' Julie said, trying to force a smile onto her face. 'Could I just ask that you get a message to Paul Margot, on the late JFK, that I've been rolled onto the LA please?' The manager nodded, writing it down on a piece of paper to go into the paperwork for Paul's flight – he didn't need to know that Julie had volunteered to be rolled.

Julie stepped out of their check-in area and into the terminal. As she walked to the gate she pulled her shoulders back and held her head high, fighting the urge to cry. She would have to draw on the strength of the old Julie to get through this, but with the old Julie came the others.

Stupid little Julie, thought you were something special, didn't you?

She wanted to scream back at them but what good would that do, and so she kept walking, refusing to listen to their spitefulness as they continued with their assault. She walked fast, feeling her body getting warmer with the exercise, and arrived minutes later at the aircraft door, just as a member of ground staff arrived escorting none other than the lead singer of her favourite band, Simon Costello. She could smell his expensive aftershave from where she stood just a few feet away from him, and she stopped in awe, taking a moment to study him now that she was so close. He wore a plain, crisp white t-shirt which showed his lean body underneath, tucked into a pair of designer jeans. His long fringe was parted in the middle in the style that was so fashionable right now, his dark blonde hair shiny and thick, wavy at the end. As she looked up to study his face, she realised that he was looking straight back at her. He looked amused, grinning at Julie with his famous smile, and suddenly she felt much better than she had just ten minutes before; the voices went quiet and she smiled back as she basked in his aura. Simon Costello was on her flight and he had smiled at her, perhaps her world hadn't just ended completely.

'Hi, I'm Julie,' she introduced herself to the flight manager in the front galley, a middle-aged man whom she had never flown with before. He looked up from the reams of paper the ground staff had just handed him. 'Ah, Julie, thanks for coming, we were already one crew down and then one of the girls got a migraine.'

Julie thought how ironic that was, and wondered if something had happened to the other girl too, whether she had faked the migraine so that she could get off and deal with something in *her* personal life. Perhaps the universe had just seen how much Julie needed saving and arranged this all for her.

'You'll be working R2, sweetheart, serving the K seats in First, is that okay?' He looked at her over the top of his glasses.

'I haven't done my First-Class training,' she said apologetically. She was due to have it soon, some of her training course had done it already, but not her.

'Oh for heaven's sake,' he complained. 'It's not your fault, love, but I specifically told them that I needed someone First Class trained, as no one else on here is.'

'I'm sorry,' Julie apologised.

'Oh, please don't say sorry,' he softened. 'If you don't mind a new challenge then we will get through it, I'll just have to train you on the job.'

'Okay, that'll be great,' Julie said with enthusiasm, a new challenge was just what she needed to take her mind off Paul. She looked down the aisle at the seats that would now be hers, and stopped when she got to Simon Costello, who was grinning at her again.

Julie loved it! The First Class service was a doddle once Keith had shown her the ropes, and with just fourteen passengers to serve between them the slower pace was such a welcome change to the chaos of Economy. She let him do the silver service, that was something that was going to need a little more practice, but overall she thought she was doing a pretty good job. With the main meal service over, Keith left her to monitor their cabin, and she walked down the aisle offering drinks and feeling like she was working on a private jet.

'Would you like a drink, sir?' Julie asked, reaching Simon and trying not to blush in his presence.

'How about your number?' he replied cheekily.

'Erm.' Julie felt her cheeks get redder, what on earth did she say to that? She knew that she was pretty, but this man was a legend and he couldn't possibly be interested in her, could he? 'I'm sorry, I don't think that would be appropriate,' she said with little conviction.

'I'd like to take you out tonight—' he paused and glanced at her name badge, 'Julie.' He wasn't giving up and Julie felt nervous flutters in her stomach.

'I bet you say that to all the girls,' she laughed, cringing as she made to walk off at her own use of such a cliché. He stopped her by grabbing her hand.

'I mean it, I really want to take you out. I've got no plans for tonight and I would really like to have someone special to eat dinner with,' he said persuasively.

Julie nearly died right there on the spot, and she struggled to keep her composure. 'I'm sorry,' was all she could muster before pulling her hand away and heading straight to the nearest toilet, the only place she could get any privacy on the plane. She took a few deep breaths and looked at herself in the mirror, holding on to the basin. Did she really have something special? Yes, she was pretty, but was there something more? Did he *really* see something? Surely, she thought, he is just after a one-night stand? And so what if he is? she reasoned, she liked sex and she really, *really* liked him… and the fact that she had a boyfriend had just recently become very insignificant.

Julie walked out of the toilet and into the galley, where she poured a single malt over ice, just how she already knew he liked it. Then she wrote her number on a napkin and took it to his seat. Setting the napkin down first she made sure that he had seen the number, before she put the glass on top and walked away. In that moment she knew what she was going to do about Paul, she was going to play him at his own game. To leave him would have meant abandoning her plan, everything she had worked for, everything she had dreamed of, and she wasn't prepared to do that… and she loved him, as much as she was hurt right now and hated what he had done, she loved him. So, she would carry on with the pretence of the perfect relationship, pretend that she didn't know what she now knew, but she wouldn't be naïve anymore. Julie Shuttleworth had just grown up.

Chapter Six

Ditching + 01:00hrs

So, what now? Julie wondered as she stood on the shore of North Hudson Bay and looked around her, small waves gently lapping up against the rafts that were now marooned half in and half out of the water. She felt her feet sinking into the boggy ground, shifting her weight from one foot to another, and looked over her shoulder at the tall trees behind them, their trunks lined up side by side like one huge fence that hid another realm behind it.

'Does anyone have a phone signal?' Iain was asking, rubbing his head with one hand while holding his own phone up in the air and waving it around with the other. No one said a word, just shook their heads and looked at their own useless gadgets. It seemed that in another stroke of bad luck they were stranded in one of the few places left on earth with no mobile phone signal. 'Well that's unfortunate, not to worry though, they will know where we are,' Iain said, too cheerfully for Julie. After the day they had just had she was going to adopt a 'hope for the best but expect the worst' attitude going forward, she had decided.

'Let's gather up the equipment and get inland a little, it's too wet here,' she suggested to Iain, still shuffling from foot to foot, but finally accepting that her shoes might not come out of this situation in their usual state of polished newness. Iain nodded in agreement and picked up the loudhailer again.

'Everyone, if I can have your attention please. We are just going to move inland and find somewhere suitable to regather.' He paused for a second before repeating Julie's other suggestion. 'Please bring with you any supplies you managed to get off the aircraft and follow me.'

'Good idea, captain,' Julie said with the dryness of the Sahara Desert. He smiled smugly and Julie turned away so that he couldn't see her roll her eyes and mouth a few choice words. Slowly, with equipment distributed between the strongest amongst them, they began to follow him in the direction of the trees, the unknown awaiting them. They were a diverse and unlikely group that needed a leader, and by default it was him; whether he was up to the job or not only time would tell.

Turning back to make sure everyone was following, Julie noticed Antonio making an arrow out of life jackets on the ground to show the rescuers which way they had gone, and she gave him a thumbs up, happy that her crew were following procedures down to the most minor of points.

Inspired, she took her own off and tied it to a tree, a minute later taking one from someone else and tying that to another a little further along, and so on. For years she had read the survival section of her manual without giving it much attention, but right now it was without a doubt the best book she had ever read.

They walked in thoughtful silence, over rocks and into the forest of huge fir-type trees. Inside its wall it was darker, and the path wasn't already trodden. Derren and the man who was still nameless from her raft, walked ahead pulling vines and branches out of the way for the rest of them, making the journey slow. Julie's senses were heightened. The noises of animals which they couldn't see startled her, and she began to feel afraid, staying close behind the two at the front as right now they seemed the most competent in the bunch.

'What the heck was that?' she gasped, louder than she had meant to, in response to a particularly chilling roar-like sound.

'A bear,' said the unnamed man indifferently, without even turning around. Julie noticed even Derren's eyes widen in reaction to this information, stalling in his work for a brief second to look at him.

'Really, are you sure? It's not just a nice deer or a fox?' she asked hopefully.

He laughed. 'No, perhaps a moose or an Arctic fox but it sounded like a bear to me. We're not in England now, my dear.'

Julie shivered. For the first time since they got off the plane she felt cold. The sun had warmed them on the raft, but now that they were shaded under the trees she could feel the drop in temperature. Somebody further back would be carrying the blankets so she could warm up soon, she hoped, this thin cardigan that the airline issued her with was barely enough onboard, let alone out here.

'Julie, nice to meet you,' she blurted out, needing the distraction of conversation.

'Ken,' he said, looking back at her and smiling. It was a nice smile, she thought. He had a calm and confident manner that made Julie want to stay close to him until this whole ordeal was over.

'If you don't mind me asking, how are you so calm?' Julie tripped over a tree root and he turned skilfully, catching her arm and saving her from falling face first into the forest floor. 'Thank you,' she said, finding her balance again and concentrating on the floor now to make sure that it didn't happen again.

'Ex-military,' he said simply, explaining everything so clearly in those two simple words.

'Ahhh, that makes sense.' Julie considered what she knew of him so far, how he didn't need to be looked after on board, how he had seen where he was needed and jumped into the freezing water to help Derren, and how he was now so subtly leading them without the captain even realising. She realised he probably had more skills than any of the crew that would help them right now, but that he was obviously enough of a gentleman, and respectful of rank, not to step on anyone's toes. 'Well don't hold back if you have any survival skills that can help us all out, feel free to take the lead,' she said, giving him the go ahead to take over the whole thing if he wanted.

'I'm sure your captain has it under control, and I know you crew have great training,' he said. 'But if you need anything I'll help where I can.'

Julie refrained from voicing her opinion on Iain's level of control. He wasn't far behind them, happy to walk the path that they had trodden, still wearing his hat and carrying nothing but his loudhailer.

'Thank you,' she said. 'Can I please have that lifejacket of yours then?'

'Certainly.' He untied his strap and slipped it over his head, giving it to Julie who promptly tied it around a tree. 'Good thinking, see, you don't need me.'

'Well we will have to agree to differ on that,' Julie said, adding an involuntary gasp as another strange noise came from the darkness.

****

Eventually the trees opened up to a sizeable clearing, sunlight reaching the ground for the first time, and Julie felt herself relax a little as she stepped into it. They all came to a stop in the centre, huddled closely together and looking at Iain, waiting for him to announce what they had already decided in their minds. Iain put his arm in the air, silencing the murmurs of conversation as if he were a religious leader, Julie thought with derision.

'Folks, we are going to stop here, it is beginning to get dark and we need to consider protection from the elements. It can get very cold out here at night time,' he said, and Julie was ever so slightly impressed that he had actually worked this one out for himself.

She nodded her head in agreement, recalling the next page in her manual:

Principles of survival:

    Protection

    Location

    Water

    Food

'Firstly, we need to do a headcount and find out what skills we have amongst us. If I could ask you to return to your raft groups, crew, please come and see me with your door number, head-counts and so on.'

Julie stepped forward immediately, as she had done her homework already. Iain took a pen out of his top pocket and fished around in his trouser pockets for some paper.

'Here.' Someone handed him a piece of paper and Julie couldn't help but be amused that it was a sick bag, the staple notepad of any flight attendant, even out here.

'Raft L1. 12 passengers, 4 crew. I plastic surgeon, 1 ex crew, 1 ex scout leader and champion den builder.' Iain raised an eyebrow and Julie shrugged. 'And one ex-military.' He nodded in approval at the last one.

'Thank you, Julie,' he said, turning to the next crew member, a young girl called Daisy who had been working in Economy. She looked pale, and was visibly shaking.

'Are you okay?' Julie asked her, putting a hand on her shoulder. Daisy shook her head and started to cry.

'Sorry, I think the adrenaline has just worn off,' she said. Julie looked around and saw that Daisy wasn't alone, that people were crying everywhere, and comforting each other. She remembered once when she was younger and crashed her car on her way to work. It was the adrenaline that had kept her moving, dealing with it all and focussing on not being late, but once she had stopped and let it sink in, the tears had come. She mentally checked on herself, realising that she felt a little wobbly too, a fluttering feeling throughout her body and her legs decidedly unsteady. But she knew that she couldn't give in to it now, she was needed by all of these people. When she got home to her flat, alone, then she would let it all come out, but not until then. She took a deep breath.

'It's okay, have a good cry but then you need to pull yourself together, you hear,' she said firmly but kindly. Falling apart wasn't going to help anyone right now. 'Remember your training, and we will be out of here in no time.'

'I don't get paid enough for this bullshit!' An angry voice came from behind her. It was Antonio, cursing in his Italian accent as he stomped towards them. 'First, they call me out on my last day of standby for this shitty flight and I missed my brother's birthday, then we ditch, and now I am being insulted by the fat woman who is personally blaming me for ruining her life!'

Julie shot her finger over her mouth to tell him to quieten down; insulting the passengers wasn't going to improve this situation one iota.

'No, I won't be quiet,' he protested. 'She just called me an imbecile because I said I didn't know when we would be rescued. It's hardly like I have a schedule of flights that rescue passengers from the middle of fucking nowhere, is it?!' His arms were flailing everywhere. 'I told her she can kiss my Italian ass, I just saved her life for fuck's sake, and she calls me stupid!'

Julie could practically see the steam coming out of his ears, and had to agree that he had a point, but you never lost your patience with a customer, ever, she had learned that the hard way. Or could they now? Was this a situation where you could give in to natural human reactions, instead of having to keep them in check? The normal working day was only as long as the flight, after all, surely she couldn't expect her crew to keep the act up indefinitely?

Iain was speechless, his pen still poised over his notepad.

'Ah sorry, captain,' Antonio said much more calmly. 'L4, 23 passengers, 1 nurse and 22 people of no use whatsoever, especially 'er, she will just need feeding too much.'

Julie gasped at this, realising that the calm Antonio that she had worked with onboard was not dealing so well with his passengers out in the wild. 'Perhaps you need a break from them, dear, stay over here for a bit until you calm down,' she said, indicating a fallen trunk on which he could sit. She could imagine the newspapers now, when the passenger told them how she was insulted by the crew, of course they wouldn't want both sides of the story. He was right though, they didn't get paid enough for this.

Eventually the information was all collated, and Iain called all of the crew together for a briefing.

'Okay, so each of you is now in charge of the passengers in your raft, make sure you know who you have and keep an eye on them. Julie, I was wondering if you could ask your military guy, and the den-builder if they can come over. Daisy, you also have ex-military, I believe?'

'Yes,' she said, seeming much brighter now, Julie was pleased to see.

'We need to get some sort of shelter built before it gets much colder, if you can all bring me anything you think we can use,' he finished.

Julie and the rest of the crew signalled their understanding and turned to head back to their areas; he was slowly going up in her estimation, but just by a little.

'Milton, Ken, the captain was wondering if you wouldn't mind helping with organising some shelter?' Milton looked positively excited, his inner scout released, and jumped to his feet immediately; the two men walked together towards where an able group of men and women were beginning to gather. 'Right, where is that canopy?' Julie asked of no one in particular, rummaging amongst the pile of supplies that had been unceremoniously dumped. Eventually she came across it in a large rubber pouch along with the inflatable poles which in theory should be put down the centre of the raft to hold the canopy up, but might just come in useful now. She took them over and handed them to Iain before walking across to the other groups to introduce herself.

From what she could see her crew had done a fantastic job. There were mounds of emergency equipment and supplies at each 'camp'. Someone from the back galley had even thrown in the crisps and chocolates from the crew cart, and a whole bag of snacks that had been left over from the drinks service. She reached Antonio, who was sitting in silence with his group, and she tried to lighten their situation by making small talk with a few, to no avail. She could see straight away the lady who he had spoken about, and immediately decided not to make the situation any worse by talking to her, as she knew someone waiting for an opportunity to vent when she saw one. If they were here much longer she would need to swap him over with somebody else, much as she would on board if a passenger took a dislike to a particular crew member, remove the source of the fire so to speak.

The next group was a complete contrast, in fact this group seemed to be quite enjoying themselves. The two girls that had been working in galley two, Nadine and Kelly, had sat themselves and their passengers next to each other and done a very good job of blending them. There was conversation, and even laughter amongst them. Julie was mesmerised for a moment, in awe of how they had made a bad situation good, until she saw the bottles of alcohol that would have been in the duty-free cart in their galley poking out from under a blanket.

Oh the trouble they were going to be in when this got to the papers, Julie cried inside. She leaned down to one of the girls who hadn't yet noticed her stood behind them.

'Nadine, I'll need to take that alcohol, I'm afraid,' she said regretfully.

Nadine turned around slowly, followed by Kelly, who was trying to move the bottle back under the blanket with her foot. Julie tried not to laugh at their obvious attempt to look innocent.

'I'm sorry, and I think I'd have done the same at your age, girls, but we can't risk someone getting drunk and out of control, or this getting to the papers, can we?'

Nadine reluctantly took the bottle of gin and handed it to Julie without saying a word.

'Thank you,' Julie said. 'Now carry on how you were, you are both doing a great job.'

Julie walked away, deliberately taking a path behind a huge tree. She quickly opened the bottle and took a huge mouthful of its precious contents, feeling the warmth as it trickled down to her stomach. She knew, of course, that there were more bottles underneath that blanket, but she wasn't the fun police, nor did she want to make a bad situation worse for anybody. Now she had done her job, dealt with what she had seen and only that, and this was her reward. One more mouthful and Julie's day felt almost wonderful, life was so much better with a gin filter, she had always thought. She looked around her for somewhere to hide the bottle, choosing a low bush with a distinctive shape; there was no way she was letting anyone else know about it as she definitely wasn't prepared to share!

Walking out from the trees Julie wondered if the gin aura that she felt around her was visible to anyone else, and the idea of it amused her as she continued with her rounds. The next group was Daisy's. It seemed that she had somehow ended up with the Chinese tour group which had been in Economy, and she was somewhat perplexed at how they had all managed to get onto the same raft, since they had been spread across the plane on both sides. All older, they seemed very sweet, smiling and nodding in reply to Julie's introductions while clearly not understanding a word. A younger member of the group, probably the tour guide, translated to them as she left.

Next, she came to the only other male crew member, Laurence, who was sitting trying to light a fire with one of his passengers. Julie had got on well with him on the flight; he was young but sure of himself, extremely handsome with the cheekiest smile, and he had teased her to the point of actually making her blush; not many boys could have got away with that, but he had.

'Good idea, Laurence, it's going to get cold tonight,' Julie said in approval.

'Are you the manager, love?' someone in his group called out to her.

'Yes, yes I am,' Julie replied humbly to the old man sitting on the floor who had spoken.

'Then you should know that this lad is an absolute hero in our eyes. The way he got us out of that aircraft, and how he's looked after us since, he deserves a medal.'

'Thank you, sir,' Julie said, feeling unexpected tears prick the back of her eyes as she swelled with pride from within; she wasn't overly familiar with this emotion, pride, but it did seem to keep catching her unawares today. 'Well done, Laurence, you're a remarkable young man, and I'm so glad you were on this flight,' she said, patting him on the shoulder.

'I'm not,' Laurence grinned. 'I would rather have been on a more straightforward one, but thank you,' he said to Julie and the man. 'Just doing what needs doing.' If Julie had ever been blessed with a son, this was the sort of boy she would have hoped to have raised.

'Well keep up the good work,' she said, smiling as she walked away.

Julie pulled her cardigan around her in an attempt to keep warm, quickly visiting the last two groups before returning to her own. She was relieved that no one had sustained any injuries, that she wasn't going to have to refer to the 'dealing with mass casualties' section of the manual while splinting limbs and applying tourniquets. Ken would possibly have been good at that though, she mused, looking over to where a very impressive shelter was being built, before taking a seat with the others on the floor.

'How are you, love?' It was Eric, sitting next to her for the second time that day, and once again saying the right thing at the right time. Julie didn't need people to look out for her, she was more than capable of looking after herself, but at a time like this everybody needed somebody to care about them. And here sat this older man, whom she had only met a few hours ago, asking her sincerely how she was.

'I'm okay, thank you,' she said with a small, grateful smile. 'I'm relieved that we all managed to get off safely,' she added.

'Yep, if I never believed in miracles before, I certainly do now,' he said. 'So, do you have a husband and children worrying about you at home?'

Julie just shook her head and bounced the question back quickly, her tried and tested method of avoiding such questions that usually worked. 'How about you two, do you have a large family?'

'Oh yes,' his wife said as she leaned over to join in. 'Five children, four girls and one boy, eight grandchildren and a great-grandchild on the way,' she said proudly.

'Wow, how lovely,' Julie said.

'Yes, we love our big family,' Bet said, smiling broadly. 'Do you have brothers and sisters? Mum and dad still?'

Julie shifted, wondering for a moment if she should just lie. 'No, it's just me,' she answered truthfully. She had stopped lying years ago, although that wasn't to say she had been entirely honest either. No one needed to know everything, because if you told them your weaknesses, they might just use them against you. Julie had learned this the hard way.

'Oh, that's terrible, love.' Eric looked visibly upset to know that she was on her own.

'Oh no, it's absolutely fine, honestly. I'm quite happy on my own,' she said brightly, trying to convince them of what she was sure of. The last thing Julie wanted was for somebody to feel sorry for her, she really didn't need their pity. She was honestly, really okay with being on her own, it was her choice after all.

'Where do you live, love?' Eric asked. She could tell that he didn't believe her protests, but she was grateful that he at least had the courtesy to change the subject.

'East London,' Julie said.

'Well so do we, there's a coincidence,' he said, his face lighting up. 'Don't you think, Bet?'

'Well I never, what a small world,' she said in agreement.

'Right, that is it,' Eric said in a tone that told Julie not to argue, 'when we get home we are going to have a barbecue at ours to celebrate, and you are going to be our guest of honour. You can come and meet the family.'

They were both looking at her with big smiles and wide eyes and Julie didn't quite know what to say.

'Oh, that's a lovely offer but…' she began feebly.

'Absolutely no buts,' Bet said firmly. 'Eric's burgers are legendary around our way, and the family will love to meet you. You must be about the same age as our Lesley. They will all love you, an extra sister.'

Julie smiled at that, a sister indeed! While she appreciated the thought, and if they were anywhere near as lovely as their parents she was sure they would all be very nice, through default she didn't do 'family gatherings'.

'Okay, okay, you've twisted my arm,' she said, just to make them happy. She would make her excuses nearer the time.

'Well that's great, as soon as we get out of here I'll get my order in with the butcher,' Eric said. 'Hopefully that won't be too long.'

They all fell silent for a moment and Julie looked around. It was nearly dark and now that they were quiet again she could hear the strange noises coming from all around them, that seemed closer than they had before. Julie shivered, from both the cold and the fear that she was trying hard to supress.

'Don't you worry, gal, we'll be out of here soon enough.' Eric put one arm around his wife and the other around Julie, squeezing her. 'And you're not on your own anymore, you're family now.'

'That's right,' agreed Bet. 'Always room for one more.'

Julie felt a little wave of gratitude, quickly brushing it aside it before she got carried away. A long time ago the offer of a family was all that she dreamed of, but not now.

Julie Margot didn't allow anyone too close, because that way she couldn't get hurt. The problem with getting hurt was that then it was hard to smile, and only while she could smile did the voices stay away.

Chapter Seven

25 years earlier

'**A**re you sure you don't want *anyone* there?' Paul asked for what must have been the umpteenth time.

'You know I don't have any family, and I don't want all of yours to spend my whole wedding day wondering why they are the only ones there,' she said, again.

'But we have friends too that I'm sure would want to come and celebrate with us.'

No, Paul, you have friends, and I have your friends, Julie corrected him in her head. She had been quite clever at disguising her lack of true friends, dropping in pretend names and phone calls occasionally. 'Paul, please, you know about my childhood, but I don't want to have to explain it to everyone else,' she pleaded, knowing that he would give in as he always did. He was the only one who did know a significant amount of her past, albeit not all, because once upon a time she had thought she could trust him with her life.

He put his arms around her and pulled her closely to him from behind as they lay on the sofa.

'You're all I need,' she said. That would always get him, he was the type of guy who needed to be needed. She doubted if they would work as a couple if she was different, if she had family and friends that took her attention away from him. He was the centre of her world, and she had a feeling that he liked it that way. She felt the familiar stir of arousal in him that those words always provoked and knew that she would now have to show him.

'Let's go to bed.' He stood up, and pulled her up too. Julie had really wanted to watch the end of the film, she had been quite enjoying it, but she followed him up the stairs obediently. She would never turn him down, she would be the perfect wife to her husband and do whatever she needed to do to keep him happy because then so would she be.

****

Three months later Julie looked out of her window onto the Las Vegas Strip, the surrealness of the millionaire's playground a good backdrop to this day in her surreal life. She turned back into the lounge area of the grand suite that most people only dreamed of staying in, and poured herself another glass of Dom Pérignon from the almost empty bottle on the glass table.

'You can come out now,' she called, ready for her appreciation.

'Wow, look at you,' Paul said, his face lighting up in approval as he came out of the bedroom.

'Well thank you,' Julie said coyly. She had found the perfect white dress that *said* 'wedding' without screaming it. Bardot style at the top and fitted to below the knee, teamed with designer crystal-encrusted shoes. The hairdresser had just left after teasing her curled hair into an exquisite updo, and the mirror had already told her that she looked good.

'You scrub up okay yourself,' she said, her husband-to-be looked dashing in his tailored three-piece suit.

'I love you, Miss Shuttleworth.' He stepped forward and leaned down to kiss her. That would be the last time she would ever be called by that name, and she couldn't wait to be rid of it.

'And I love you too, Mr Margot,' she kissed him back. She smiled as she said it, she wasn't lying, and she knew that he wasn't either. She had been flying for five years now, and she had seen enough pilots, and indeed crew, shag around on their layover and then tell you all about their wonderful family in the flight deck on the way home. Some people just couldn't say no when it was handed it to them on a plate, they were weak. In contrast, *she* was strong, everything Julie Shuttleworth did was for a purpose, and Julie Margot would be no different. So, she would turn a blind eye to his indiscretions, and occasionally she might have her own if she needed to, because that gave her back control without him even knowing it.

'Right, let's go get married,' he announced. Julie finished the last mouthful of her champagne, putting the empty glass back on the table and picking up her small clutch bag. She felt butterflies of excitement in her stomach which made her whole face stretch into the biggest smile she had ever produced. Paul took her hand and she practically skipped out of the room behind him, eager to turn the page onto the next chapter in her life.

Downstairs the driver held open the door of the convertible limousine and she shrieked in excitement as they drove down the Strip, past all of the huge hotels with their flashing lights and neon signs. She turned occasionally to look at Paul, exchanging kisses and holding hands until they arrived at the chapel.

Inside, the Elvis impersonator welcomed them with a rendition of 'Love Me Tender', and in front of him and two strangers wearing shorts and flip flops they promised to love and honour each other. Only she knew that Paul was hiding his infidelities, he thought that she was faithful to him in every way, and for a fleeting moment she hoped that it made him feel just a little bit bad.

Afterwards, at the 'Welcome to Las Vegas' sign he lifted her into the air as the limo driver took their picture and showed all the tourists there how much he loved her, and then he took her back to their suite and they made love as man and wife. As he lay asleep that night Julie got up and went into the bathroom. She smiled at her reflection, at Julie Margot, captain's wife. She wondered if her mother would have been proud of her, or her dad, whoever and wherever he was. She wished that she had someone to share her glory with. But she did have Paul, and he would have to be enough, indeed if she hadn't spoken to Lisa on that day two years ago she could have believed that he was everything she could ever want. She felt sad for her loss, sad that her bubble had been burst. She wanted to love him like she had on that morning, back when she hadn't felt alone for the first time in her life. She looked through the door into the bedroom where he lay quietly sleeping. No, she wasn't alone, he did love her, or why else would he have married her? She just needed to be a little bit wary, that was all, save a little bit for herself just in case things went wrong.

Julie opened her wash bag and took out her contraceptive pills, popping them out one by one into the toilet and flushing them away. Now she needed him to give her a baby, to bond them with something unbreakable. She felt a warmth as she thought of having her own child, someone that she could love unconditionally and who would love her back the same because she would be the best mum in the world. That was the next part of her plan, the first chapter in the story of Julie Margot.

Julie climbed back into bed and wrapped her arms around her husband. It felt good and she fell asleep full of excitement for her future.

Chapter Eight

Ditching + 04:00hrs

A new noise in the distance got Julie's attention, a humming sound that was definitely getting closer, she decided. The hubbub of conversation in the camp tailed off as it got louder and louder.

'It's a plane,' someone yelled, and everyone but no one sprung to their feet and started looking to the darkening sky. Yells of 'Down here!' and 'Over here!' reverberated off the trees around them as they all frantically tried to get the pilot's attention. They couldn't hear them though, the small plane circling a way off, and never quite getting close enough to notice them in their clearing in the trees. Julie was sure they must have seen the rafts on the edge of the lake, that they would know people had managed to get off the plane. She wondered how deep the lake was, and if the plane's transponder would still be transmitting. A whooshing sound made her turn and she watched as a flare launched into the air, bursting into bright red light high above their heads. Antonio stood at its source, holding the empty vessel in which it had been held for all those years inside of the raft that was never truly supposed to be used.

It was silent now as everyone held their breath, joining forces in their thoughts to will the pilot to see the light and turn back around, but he didn't, the hum of the plane's propeller getting quieter and quieter as it flew away.

'They'll be back,' called the captain, and Julie was glad of the reassurance. 'We just have to let them know where we are. But for now, we need to get us safe for the night, God knows what's out here.'

Julie thought he looked nervous as he looked around him, scared of the dark perhaps, or of the things it might hide.

'Ladies and gentlemen, it may not be five-star but I'm sure you will agree these fine people have created a pretty good shelter for us,' he announced.

They all looked over to the huge tent that had been erected, and Julie was quite awestruck now that she had a proper look at it. The raft canopies had been draped over the boughs of trees to give it height and it was reinforced around the edges by the inflatable supports she had provided. There was a doorway at one end, Milton standing next to it like a tour guide, holding the flap open, eager to show them his work.

'Right, well this is the living area,' he began as they followed him inside. Everyone was silent as they listened intently to him talk about their accommodation on this spontaneous camping trip. Julie thought she could imagine him giving presentations in business meetings by the confident and engaging way in which he spoke. The floor was lined with more of the plastic canopies and she considered whether she should suggest that people take their shoes off so that they could keep some level of cleanliness, deciding quickly that an air disaster warranted the dropping of all such standards.

'Over here we have designated sleeping areas.' Milton walked over to the back where three small rooms, so to speak, jutted off the sides. They had been built under the low branches at the edge of the clearing and so were not high enough to stand in, but with the accompanying darkness they did remind her somewhat of crew rest. 'And that area over there is for equipment stowage.' He pointed to a corner on the opposite side where a lot of the equipment had already been piled up in need of some serious sorting. The rest of the tent was just one large room, big enough for all of them to sit or lie, and to shelter together until they were found. Julie was impressed.

'Well, ladies and gentlemen, if you'd like to make yourselves as comfortable as possible,' Iain interrupted, 'crew, if we could just get together for a moment.' The passengers dispersed, leaving the two pilots and nine crew alone for the first time since the briefing back in Seattle all that time ago. 'So, can I suggest, crew, that you and your teams gather up any other equipment you have and bring it on in. Milton has offered to help with the camp fire outside, we will need it quite a lot bigger for warmth and to put off any wildlife. We will need to organise a three-hour watch of course, and get a beacon on the go if anyone managed to get one off.'

'Can I suggest each raft takes turns to nominate people for a watch, Iain,' Julie suggested, slightly put out that he was getting ahead of her now. 'And perhaps we could arm them with crash axes just in case of bears?'

'Yes, that's a good idea, Julie,' he agreed, and she was glad that he hadn't found the last suggestion ridiculous. The small axes were carried for various purposes onboard, but she was sure that until now, fighting bears wasn't one of them.

Julie wandered out of the tent, looking around for someone to help her with her own equipment. She found Ken outside talking to Milton as they piled wood up to build the fire which Laurence had successfully started.

'Ken, could you possibly help me gather our things together?' she asked politely.

'Of course,' he replied and walked beside her to where they had left their equipment. Once there he held out his strong arms and Julie commenced to pile things up on top on them. Blankets, radio beacon, raft survival pack, crash axe, first aid kit, makeup bag… Julie looked up sheepishly at Ken and took it back from the top of the pile that nearly reached his eyes. She wondered if he recognised it for what it was, before that thought was swiftly replaced by the one of how dreadful she must look right now. She raised her hand and felt her hair, stray ends sticking out everywhere, and wished she had thrown in a hairbrush too.

'Right, that should do it,' she said, gathering up the last few things and looking around one final time, noticing a light shining on the floor a few feet away. She was pleased to find it was coming from one of the aircraft's emergency torches, which lit up automatically when they were removed from their stowage. Now that she looked, she could see several other torch lights scattered about in the heavy blanket of darkness that was descending so fast now. She collected them up quickly, glad of their brightness and that of the flames coming from the bonfire too. Julie had never been camping as a child, and certainly never fancied it as an adult, but as they walked back with their cargo she couldn't help thinking that they were quite well equipped, everything considered.

Back in the tent Iain and Derren were busy organising the equipment, and people had spread themselves evenly around. She noticed that the passengers from her raft had stayed together, as had the other groups, and couldn't help smiling at the fact that the teams had been formed out there on the water, and were very much cemented already.

'We'll take first watch, Iain,' Julie said, looking at the time on her watch. It was just after one in the morning at

82

home, and she wondered what time it was in this zone they were in now. 'My men are out there sorting the fire anyway.'

'Good call.' Iain looked up from the radio beacon he was trying to fathom out.

'Just pull the toggle to ON and it works automatically for a minimum of forty-eight hours, transmitting a signal every fifty seconds,' she said smugly as she walked away, but he didn't answer.

'How is everyone?' Julie asked as she reached her group. They all looked exhausted and uncomfortable on the hard ground, with just a few blankets between them. They smiled back at her though, no one complained.

'I don't suppose there is any water?' Chloe asked quietly.

'She needs to drink plenty because she's feeding Reuben,' Luke added apologetically.

'Yes, yes, of course, I'm so sorry, you poor girl.' Julie could see how dry and cracked her lips were already, and she realised how long it must have been since any of them had drunk anything. 'I'll get you some water.' She hurried back over to the equipment area where she had seen some earlier, both pouches from the survival kits and bottles that some clever crew had thrown in their rafts. Julie considered adding her makeup to the supplies, quite a few of the ladies could benefit from it, after all, it always made her feel much more positive when she had her face on.

'Derren, can you pass me a bottle of that water please,' she asked.

'Oh, sorry, Julie, we need to ration that out, only for the sick and the elderly at the moment I'm afraid.'

'Well I have a breastfeeding mother who needs it, thank you very much.' Julie reached past him and snatched a bottle away. She was well aware of the need to ration the water and he should know that she was. Did he think she was just taking it because she fancied a drink? She huffed as she walked off.

'Now we don't have too much so make that last you, but we need to keep Mummy hydrated don't we.' Julie found herself talking to the little boy who was staring up at her, captivating her. His big sky-blue eyes seemed to be talking back to her and she was mesmerised.

'Do you want to hold him?' Chloe was holding him out and before Julie could refuse he gave her a huge grin and she couldn't resist. She sat on the floor, afraid she might drop this precious bundle.

'I think he likes you,' Chloe said, sipping the water.

'I like you very much too,' Julie cooed, stroking the side of his face lightly. 'Lovely to meet you, little Reuben, I'm Julie.' Reuben smiled again and Julie melted.

'Shame you never had kids, love, you'd have made a lovely mum.' It was Eric.

'Ah, it just wasn't for me, Eric,' Julie said. She knew he was trying to be nice but it wasn't something she wanted to go into, with anyone. Julie handed Reuben back to Chloe, the moment quashed by the well-meant comment. 'Thank you for letting me hold him, he's adorable,' she said, getting up and excusing herself. As she stepped outside of their circle she glanced over to where little Ruby lay with her head on Anna's lap, covered in a blanket. They were talking quietly to each other and giggling, while Anna stroked her hair back, sharing something special. So that was how a mother was supposed to look at her daughter, Julie thought. She couldn't remember her own mother ever looking at her like that.

A blanket wrapped around her shoulders and a torch in her hand, Julie stepped outside and walked over to the fire that was burning nicely now.

'You two have been nominated for first watch, have you seen any bears?' she asked nervously.

'A couple, but we saw them off with our axe,' Ken said, with a grin that told her they hadn't. 'We might try to catch the next one for dinner though.'

'Oh, why did you have to mention dinner?' Milton groaned. 'I'm bloody starving.'

'Yes, sorry, no one thought to cater us for an extra night,' Julie apologised dryly. She was somewhat hungry too, but that was the least of her worries.

'Worst airline I've ever flown with,' Ken tutted, still grinning. Julie enjoyed the banter, he was easy to get along with, they both were.

'Be sure to fill in your survey, and fly with someone else next time,' she retorted.

'Someone else? I'm never getting on a plane again as long as I live, I'm terrified!' He and Milton were laughing now and it was infectious. Julie couldn't help but join in, just for a moment.

'Now if you can just try and take the situation seriously, gentlemen, we are relying on you to protect the camp.'

'Geez, boss, that's one hell of a responsibility to take on with nothing but this.' Ken held up the axe which did look somewhat ridiculous now, small with a red head that was only ever meant to smash the flight deck window or make a hole in the aircraft panelling. They were off laughing again but Julie couldn't join in this time. It wasn't in her nature to be spontaneous, to let herself really go, despite how amusing it was to watch these big grown men laugh like young boys.

Walking back to the tent Julie stopped and looked back to the fire; the men hadn't even noticed that she had gone as they larked about. Even with their hysterics, she felt safe knowing that they were keeping watch, that they would be capable of fending off any bears. Milton disappeared behind the fire and she took a brief moment to study Ken properly for the first time. He wasn't the biggest man she had ever seen, perhaps just under six feet tall, but without even setting eyes on the muscles that were suggested underneath his shirt she could just tell he was exceptionally strong, both in his body and in his mind. She turned back, bumping into Chloe and Luke as they came out of the tent.

'Julie, Chloe needs a wee,' Luke said. She loved how he was looking out for her, worrying about her, even speaking for her.

'Here take this, I'm afraid the facilities are a little basic,' she said, handing Luke the torch.

'Would you mind watching Reuben?' Chloe asked, passing him to Julie. Once again, he was in her arms before she could say no, and she wondered if anyone ever considered that not everyone liked babies. Of course, it wasn't exactly that she didn't like babies, Reuben was quite sweet as far as they went, but she had absolutely no idea what to do with one.

As the light of the torch disappeared into the woods, the pair of them swallowed up by the darkness, Reuben's little face crumpled and Julie realised that he was about to cry. Terrified and rooted to the spot, she willed them to come back immediately. Too late, he made a small sound and let out a wail, everyone within earshot turning to see her stood there, holding a baby with a look of complete panic on her face. Julie jostled him in her arms, she had seen people rock them like this before, and she tried that to no avail. Next, she put him on her shoulder and patted his back, she had seen that too… but he was just getting louder. In desperation she brought him back down and began to sing, a song by her favourite band, not even a lullaby, but she didn't know any of those… and the crying stopped. Reuben stared at her and she laughed at his puzzled expression.

'You like that song?' she asked, before carrying on. She could feel herself smiling as he stared back at her, his expression relaxing, herself relaxing in response, and then his eyes closed as he fell off to sleep.

'We're back,' Chloe said as they came back inside. 'Has he been okay?'

'He's been an angel,' Julie said, handing back the sleeping baby. Maybe Eric was right, maybe she would have been a good mum, but she hadn't allowed herself to think about that for many years now.

Chapter Nine

21 years earlier

'Julie are you ready?' Paul sounded impatient.

'Just coming,' Julie called back down. 'Won't be a second.'

She took one last look in the mirror, pleased with how the dress looked, at how it accentuated her bust and made her waist look tiny, and she hoped that Paul would like it.

Holding on to the handrail she walked carefully down the wide staircase of their beautiful home, waiting for him to turn around and see her from where he stood at the door.

'Come on for God's sake, the taxi is waiting,' he barked without even looking around.

Julie put on her coat and followed him through the front door and into the waiting taxi. Paul climbed into the front passenger seat; he hadn't so much as noticed her dress or the effort she had made for him. It was all for him after all, there was no one else she needed.

Oh dear, poor Julie Shuttleworth is losing her man.

He's going to leave you, and then where will you be?

You couldn't give him a baby so he's going to find someone who can!

The voices, oh the voices were back, and nothing she could do would make them stop. She stared out of the taxi window as they drove past streets of houses much smaller than hers, but somehow happier, with Christmas trees lit up in the windows. She wondered if the people inside were happy, loved, planning a Christmas with their children and families, like she had hoped to be.

The taxi turned into the long driveway that led up to Paul's parents' house, and she pulled herself together. This *was* a Christmas with family, Paul's family were hers now after all, but why did she never quite feel like she belonged?

Because you don't belong, why would they want you to be part of their family?

You aren't good enough!

'Thank you.' Paul was paying the taxi driver and Julie put a smile on her face. Once upon a time he would have opened the door for her, but she knew better than to wait for him now, and she got out of the car.

'Do I look okay?' she asked him, opening her coat to show her dress, making him look at her, drawing out the compliment that she so needed.

'Yes, you look fine, stop fussing, it's only my parents,' he said, barely looking at her. Julie felt the twinge of rejection, sadness even, that had been getting all too familiar lately. She tied the belt back around her coat and walked dejectedly behind him to the front door.

'Come on in!' Paul's dad bellowed, opening it wide to let them past. 'Everyone is out back.' Julie leaned in and kissed him on the cheek as she always did.

'Let me take your coat, my dear,' he offered as he closed the door.

'Thank you.' Julie took it off and handed it to him.

'Well I must say you look spectacular this evening,' he said, and he looked her up and down. Julie felt herself blush.

'Thank you.' She turned to see if Paul had heard, but was disappointed to see he had already abandoned her and headed into the dining room to greet everybody.

'Let me have the pleasure of escorting you,' John said, offering her his arm. Julie liked his dad. He had the charm born from years in the military, and was still very handsome, looking just like an older version of his son. Their own relationship was strained though, Paul's childhood tainted by his father's philandering apparently, and the irony wasn't lost on Julie.

91

Julie took his arm and walked down into the large dining room where people stood around the beautifully decorated table for their traditional pre-Christmas gathering, working her way around the room to say hello to everyone.

'Cocktail?' Paul's brother Brian handed her a martini.

'Wonderful, thank you,' Julie said, taking a sip and appreciating the immediate warmth it gave her. She had managed to sneak a couple of gins in before they left too, the Dutch courage that she had come to rely on a lot lately.

'You are looking rather lovely this evening, Julie,' Brian complimented her, and Julie smiled gratefully in acceptance. Paul was standing on the other side of the room so had missed this compliment too, but it didn't matter, Julie had the confidence boost that she needed from two people now, and she was determined to enjoy the evening from here on.

'And so does your wife,' Julie teased, looking over to his plain but lovely wife, Paula.

'Yes, she does,' he nodded, 'but we can't all strike as lucky as my brother did.'

Julie wasn't stupid, she knew he was flirting with her, the same as his dad was. She wasn't family to them at all, she was just Paul's trophy wife, something to be won.

Sitting between Paul's mother, Vera, and Paula for the extravagant four-course meal, she found the evening tolerable. She knew that both John and Brian were watching her, and their interest, coupled with the wine, was making her play up to them. She smiled broader, tossing her head back when she laughed, and the more she acted at having the best time, the more she really did.

'More wine?' John worked his way around the table topping up people's glasses.

'Dad.' Julie looked to the other end of the table where Paul had chosen to sit and saw him giving his dad a stern look while shaking his head subtly. Julie wondered what was going on until she noticed the wine bottle suspended over her glass, and then pulled away without anything being poured. She looked up at John who seemed embarrassed and moved on to his wife, topping up her glass and moving swiftly on again to the next person.

Julie felt her cheeks burning crimson. She was embarrassed, and wondered if everyone had seen what had just happened. She looked down at her plate and pushed the food around on it with her fork; her appetite had just been well and truly quashed. She couldn't look up, she was afraid to see if anyone was looking at her, if they had seen her husband just shame her like that. She wasn't drunk, merry maybe, but so was everybody, so why on earth had he just made a spectacle out of her like that? Had she been too loud? No, Paula and Vera had been loving her stories about her layovers, hadn't they?

You were making a fool of yourself as usual

You were drunk, you're always drunk!

No, she wasn't! Julie argued back. She liked a drink, everybody in her job did, Paul just didn't like her getting attention, that was all. Well perhaps if he gave her just an ounce of it, she wouldn't need it from elsewhere.

'So, what are you two doing for Christmas?' Vera was asking her a question and she reluctantly looked up from her plate.

'We are both flying, unfortunately,' Julie said.

'Somewhere nice though?' Paula was looking at her with an expectant smile.

'I'll be in LA, and Paul will be in New York.'

'Oh, that's a shame you won't be together,' Vera said sympathetically.

'Yes, it is.' Julie had once hoped for a nice Christmas together, but Paul hadn't seemed in the slightest bit bothered that they would be apart, nor had he made any effort that she knew of to get on her flight. After feeling rejected for some months now, despite her best efforts at being the perfect wife, she wasn't about to swap onto his. 'It's an occupational hazard, I'm afraid, we've been like passing ships lately.'

'Yes, well I spent years of John being away for months on end, but it isn't forever.' Vera had laid her hand on Julie's and was looking at her with true kindness. 'Once you have children it will be different, you'll see. Then only one of you will be flying off and you'll have much more time together.'

Julie felt the punch in her stomach, right where her useless womb was. For four years she had tried to get pregnant, but nothing, and now she never would because Paul didn't come anywhere near her anymore.

'Excuse me, I just need the ladies' room.' Julie pushed her cutlery together on her plate and smiled sweetly as she got up. In the bathroom she wept, allowing the tears that she had held back for so long to come out. She knew that she had lost control of her life, but the question was, what was she going to do about it? She took a deep breath as she digested the question. So things weren't going according to her plan, but was she going to just sit by and let Paul treat her like this before dropping her like a piece of rubbish and moving on to the next girl. He probably already had her lined up, it would explain his coldness.

Poor, poor Julie, dumped and left on the shelf. No one will want you now!

Yes they will, they do! Julie screamed back, defying the voices. She was still beautiful, and she knew that most men would love to have her on their arm. Paul was the weak one, not her, he was just like his father, needed to screw around to feed his ego, but *she* was in control. *She* didn't *need* to cheat on him to make herself feel better. No, she knew she was enough, she did whatever she did to stay in control, she needed to be in control.

Leaving the bathroom she walked downstairs and into the kitchen, finding John there alone.

'Ah, Julie, I'm so sorry about my son, let me get you a drink, our secret.' He tapped the side of his nose with his finger and poured a large gin and tonic into a glass for her.

'Why thank you, John,' she said, blinking more than was necessary and smiling seductively at him.

****

'Where have you two been?' Vera asked when Julie and John came back into the room.

'Julie was just helping me in the kitchen, dear.' John leaned over and placed the enormous board of cheeses, grapes and crackers that they had just thrown together in the middle of the table.

'Thank you, Julie, it looks wonderful,' Vera gushed. Julie was glad of her First-Class training and how she could make something look wonderful in seconds, as she had been busy helping John with other things the rest of the time.

'Oh, you're welcome, Vera, my pleasure,' she said sweetly.

As everyone dived into the cheese and biscuits, guzzling John's vintage port to wash it down, Julie looked across the table and exchanged a knowing look with him. No one would ever know what had just passed between them, but *she* knew, and that was enough.

Chapter Ten

Ditching + 13:30hrs

Julie's neck hurt and she turned her head in an effort to ease it – the floor was so hard here in the back galley. She shifted onto her other side but it didn't help, she would have to get up even though she felt so tired, others might be able to sleep here when there was no crew rest area but it definitely wasn't for her. She could hear voices, they were low but familiar to her, and she opened one eye slowly, wanting to see the galley around her but deep down knowing that she wasn't going to, that she was dreaming.

It was hazy, everything veiled in a grainy darkness, but a slight hint of daylight was seeping through the canopy above her and her stomach sank when she remembered where she was. Julie hauled her stiff body up, surprised and touched to find she was covered in a man's suit jacket. Her team were gathered around her, everyone seemed to be asleep; Eric and Bet were sleeping sitting up with their backs against the tent wall, supported by a tree or something behind it. Eric's arm was around his wife as she rested her head on his chest. Little Ruby was still lying in her mum's lap, and Chloe and Luke lay side by side with Reuben between them, all sharing his blankets. The others lay singly around, although she couldn't see Brian and Ken, and suspected they were still outside. No one had left the group to sleep in the designated rooms, it seemed that they were firmly sticking together.

Julie was thirsty, and she knew everyone else would be the same too when they woke up, it had been so long since they had anything to eat or drink. Quietly she crept over to the supplies. Derren lay in front of them with his eyes closed, and in that moment she wanted to just grab what she could and run like a feral child, someone she knew a long, long time ago. She stopped short as Derren opened his eyes.

'I wasn't asleep,' he mumbled, sitting up.

'It's okay if you were,' Julie said warmly. 'Derren, we need to divide up this water, everyone is going to need some today.'

'I'll see what the captain says.'

Derren's answer riled Julie, especially since she had already passed Iain snoring loudly just now, and pilots were always happy to leave her to deal with catering and passengers at any other time.

Ditched

'Well in his absence I am sure we can decide a fair way to distribute it,' she said tersely, stepping over him.

Julie looked over the jumbled piles, soon seeing the familiar blue leather pouches that she had been looking for. Before every flight she checked that one of these was at her door, but never had she opened one, until now. Pulling the yellow plastic seal to break it she undid the zip to reveal the pouches of water inside. It wasn't a lot, but it would certainly get them through the next twenty-four hours, and she hoped that would be enough.

'I suggest each crew-member is given one kit, one per raft, and that anyone with over twenty people gets an extra bottle of water,' she said, looking at the dozen or so water bottles thrown in one corner. 'That will have to last them today, and we will keep the rest of the bottles just in case we have an extra night here.'

Derren nodded. 'I agree, good plan.'

'See, we didn't need four stripes to work that one out,' Julie smiled at him.

She carried her heavy pouch back over to her group, leaving Derren to distribute the rest, and laying it down at the edge. She liked the quietness, like on a night flight when you had time before they all woke up for breakfast to have a coffee and do your makeup. She yearned for a coffee, before realising that the second part of her thought was entirely possible, pulling out her makeup bag from where she had semi-hidden it under the tent's side. She sat in the half-light with her mirror, and once she had gotten over the shock of how dreadful she looked, began applying a new layer to her face; yes she was tired, like she was at the end of every flight, but there was no need to look like it.

Five minutes later she was able to smile back at her reflection; she was aware that she had applied it in bad lighting, but an expert like her could do it in the dark. Now she was ready for them all to wake up and greet them with that flight attendant smile which she always wore for passengers; yesterday she had perhaps worn it less, but today was a new day.

Julie stepped outside to find quite a group of men standing around the fire, which was still burning brightly. They were all stood close to its heat, probably because none of them seemed to be wearing jackets despite the chill in the air, and she went back inside to retrieve the one that had been loaned to her. She glanced around and saw that several of the others seemed to have been covered up by these kind men too.

'Good morning, gentlemen,' Julie said brightly, holding up the jacket. 'I believe this may belong to one of you.'

'That's mine, thank you.' Milton reached out and took it from her.

'No, thank *you*, Milton, that was very kind of you,' she looked at the others, 'and of all of you, I presume you have all done the same.'

'We kept warm out here with the fire,' one of them said.

'You must have been busy keeping it going?' Julie asked.

'Well there's no shortage of wood around here,' said Ken. 'We heard a plane a while back, but it was a bit far off. We hoped they might see the fire.'

'It is nearly daylight, I'm sure they will find us soon enough,' Julie said, hoping that she was right. 'You must all be tired, I can arrange someone else to come out and take over?'

'I'm good,' Ken said, and Julie had to admit he did look okay. In the morning light she noticed the grey flecks in his hair and stubble and wondered how old he was. His smile and his sparkling, kind blue eyes had the youth of a twenty-year-old, but the lines that etched his weathered skin put him into his fifties, she thought.

'Me too,' added Milton. 'I could murder a coffee though.'

'Oh me too, but the best I can offer is water I'm afraid,' Julie apologised, almost able to smell the aroma of coffee in the air, so strong was her longing for it now. 'Your crew members will each have rations for your groups.'

'Rations, wow,' Ken smirked. 'It's like being at war.'

'Hopefully just for today,' Julie said. 'I'm going to go and wake the captain up and see about getting us out of here.'

Julie walked back into the tent purposefully. The daylight had arrived quickly, and people were now beginning to move around. Iain was still snoring, but Julie prodded him anyway – if he wanted to be a hero then he had to act like one.

'What?' he mumbled.

'It's time to get up,' Julie said in her bossiest voice. 'Those men have kept watch and kept that fire burning all night, now they need a plan.'

Iain sat up and for a second Julie saw the young boy inside of him, the one that lived inside every man, a bewildered look on his face. 'Iain, we need a crew brief,' she said, giving him some direction. 'Derren and I have already decided how to dish out the water supplies, but we don't have enough to survive here for long, and since it seems the planes can't see us here amongst these trees, we need to sort out a plan to get help.'

'Yes, yes.' Iain was on his feet now, as if she had been his sergeant major giving him his orders. 'Gather the crew up and we will have a brief.'

Julie nodded, agreeing to her own plan.

Ten minutes later the crew sat around in various levels of alertness, waiting for Iain to tell them what they were going to do. 'Would anyone like any of this?' Julie held up her makeup bag. 'Absolutely no pressure, grooming standards don't apply here, but I know I feel better when I don't look dreadful.' She was pleased to see all of the girls put their hands up, and passed the bag to Jody, who sat on her left, with a sense of satisfaction. 'Pass it around, dear.'

Soon Iain arrived with Derren, launching straight into 'his' plan about rationing the water and needing to find help, Julie was getting used to him hijacking her ideas now and shrugged it off.

'Now for the next thing, we need to find help, and in the event that we can't find it quickly, we need to find water, and then food.'

'I brought snacks,' said Antonio.

'Us too,' offered Nadine. Julie suddenly remembered the alcohol they had brought, and more importantly the gin that she had hidden. The desire for coffee was swiftly replaced by one for gin.

'Well let's divide that out like we did the water,' Iain continued. 'So I suggest Derren and I go off and look for help. I'm sure we can't be far from a road or something.'

'Perhaps three people would be better,' interrupted Julie. 'In case someone gets injured.' It was in the manual, always threes. She thought it was strange that he was suggesting both of the pilots leave together, but since their skills were largely redundant here anyway she decided not to comment on that. Perhaps it would be nice to actually be in charge, and get the credit for her own ideas going forward...

'Okay, three people,' Iain conceded. 'Julie, I will leave you and the crew here to look after the passengers. Now, if someone could bring me a suitable volunteer, and meet us at the equipment store so that we can see what is of use to us there.' Julie decided there and then that she would not be volunteering any of her group, she needed them all, one of the others was bound to have someone more disposable.

'Maybe we could take a raft back out onto the water so that any planes can spot us?' suggested Jody.

'That would be a great idea, but without any means of controlling its direction, and no paddles, it's probably safer to stay on land,' Derren pointed out kindly.

'Oh, and gather up any phones you can, different networks if possible, if anyone has any battery left.' Iain took his own phone out of his pocket and shook his head disappointedly at it.

****

Within an hour, just as the day finished breaking, they were gone, and the camp was quiet as everyone reflected on what would happen now. Julie felt hungry and knew that the others would be too, seeing their eyes light up as she approached them with a bag of snacks.

'It's not much, but it's something,' she said as she handed each person a small bag of crisps and a pouch of water. 'You'll need to make the water last the day though,

I'm afraid, but hopefully we will be out of here by lunchtime anyway,' she added brightly.

'I'm so hungry, Mom,' Julie heard Ruby say sadly.

'Here, you can have mine too, sweetheart, I don't like them,' Julie lied, handing the little girl her own packet much to the disgust of her rumbling stomach.

'Thank you,' she said sweetly.

'And you can have mine too, but don't be thinking you can have chips for breakfast when we get home,' Anna said with a smile, making her daughter giggle.

'Would you like crisps?' Julie offered Cheryl. She was sitting with her knees up in front of her, hugging her long slim legs. Her head was bowed and she didn't even look up, just shook it.

'I'll have hers then,' Phil interjected. Julie felt instantly annoyed, that this man was prepared to eat two bags of crisps when she and Anna had just sacrificed theirs. She looked at the bulge of his stomach and saw an ugliness in him that she hadn't noticed before.

'Cheryl, are you sure, even if you save them for later?' Julie coaxed, ignoring Phil. She had crouched down in front of her now and waited for her to look up. 'Cheryl?'

'Leave her, love, she's in one of her moods,' Phil said and his unkind tone made him uglier still. It had an effect though, and for just a second Cheryl raised her head, if only to throw him an evil look. As she turned her face to the side Julie noticed the faded bruise that had emerged around her eye now that her makeup had worn off. She felt the heat rise up her neck and clenched her teeth together.

'I'll hang on to them in case you want them later,' she said, rising to her feet and trying to maintain her composure as she walked away. So that was Cheryl's problem – Phil. Julie watched her from a distance, keeping her head down, obviously ashamed to let anyone see her bruises. Maybe he had told her to hide them, she thought, though it was he who should be truly ashamed after all, and she watched him with venom as he got up and walked across the tent to go outside. Julie took a deep breath and calmed herself down, seeing an opportunity to help, without crossing any lines. She approached Cheryl cautiously and crouched down, beside her this time, leaning in to speak so that she couldn't be overheard.

'Cheryl, I thought you may like to borrow this, I've been passing it around to all the ladies, a girl always likes to look her best,' she said, placing the makeup bag beside her. Cheryl's head turned slightly to see what it was and Julie stood back up, walking away without saying any more.

****

'Thank you.'

Julie looked up from where she had been sitting playing charades with Ruby. Cheryl was there holding out the bag, no sign of the bruise on her face.

'Oh you are very welcome,' she said, getting up and taking back the precious bag, happy to see that her idea had worked. 'My makeup really suits you.'

Cheryl smiled and for the first time Julie saw how attractive she was under her hard shell. They were probably about the same age, but Cheryl had definitely had the benefits of free plastic surgery, her skin tight and no sign of the jowls that Julie had been noticing on herself lately. 'I feel almost human now, if only you had some gin the day would be almost perfect,' she added wistfully, looking around at her surroundings.

'Well it just so happens—' Julie took Cheryl's hand and quickly led her out of the tent. Minutes later she pulled the bottle from under the bush and held it up triumphantly.

'Here to serve,' she said with a huge grin and handed it to a visibly surprised and extremely grateful Cheryl. It only took a few mouthfuls before they were both on par and smiling despite the situation. They didn't talk much but there was an unspoken understanding between them that Julie knew about Cheryls' bruises, and that it was clear where they had come from.

'You are very kind, Julie, I'm sorry if I was rude to you at all. It's easier not to say anything to people then I can't say the wrong thing, so I just let him do all the talking,' she said without emotion.

'Oh, believe me I've had much worse rude passengers, and I understand, you do not need to apologise,' Julie said, taking one last sip and screwing the lid back on. 'We'd better save some for later, our secret,' she winked.

'It's safe with me. I'd better get back before Phil starts getting twitchy, he doesn't like not knowing where I am.' Cheryl was looking around her with a vacant expression, and Julie could sense that she would much rather stay here, drinking gin together. She put her hand gently on her arm.

'I might be overstepping the mark, but I know a controlling man when I see one. You are a beautiful, strong woman, and you can survive without him, if that is what you want to do.' Instinctively she put her arms around her and hugged her quickly.

'Thank you,' Cheryl said, pulling back. 'I think this whole situation might have given me the wakeup call I needed, perhaps I'll leave the bastard when we get out of here.'

'Well I have a spare room in London if you need somewhere to escape to,' Julie offered, surprising herself that she actually meant it, that she was inviting someone to stay in her apartment, that she had just hugged that someone, and that… well, that she had acted so *differently* to her usual guarded self. She liked how it made her feel, even if it came with risks. 'Here.' She unscrewed the lid of the gin again, taking a large medicinal gulp to stop herself overthinking what had just happened and handing the bottle back to Cheryl. 'One last dose of Dutch courage.'

Cheryl took a sip and handed it back to Julie, who screwed the lid on for the second time. 'Julie,' she said with a thoughtful look on her face, 'I think you may have just saved my life for the second time.'

This time it was Cheryl who hugged Julie, and Julie hoped that she really had helped this lady choose a different path, to let go of the fear and go into the unknown when they got out of here. It might be quite fun to have a flat mate, she thought, especially one that shared her love of gin.

Chapter Eleven

19 years earlier

'**D**on't you walk away from me,' Paul shouted, pulling her from behind by her hair and making her fall to the ground. 'Get up!'

Julie stood up – she could feel that her legs were shaking, she wanted to run but she had nowhere to go.

'How fucking dare you show me up in front of my friends.' He was drunk.

'I didn't do anything,' Julie said feebly. She looked at her husband in front of her and wondered where the man who had once loved her had disappeared to. 'Please, Paul, I'm sorry.'

She didn't know what she was apologising for. They had been out with his friends and she hadn't even had a drink, Paul had stopped her drinking when they went out together a long time ago, even though it was he who had developed quite a serious drinking problem. She had only spoken to the women too, since talking to men had been the cause of previous outbursts like this. She should have been angry at his hypocrisy but she was too broken for that.

'Showing off like that, laughing at their dumb jokes.'

So that was it, she must have smiled when his friends were making him the butt of their jokes. But everyone was laughing, it was just banter, and she would have looked pretty miserable if she had kept a straight face.

'Oh for heaven's sake, is that what you are upset about?'

As she said it she knew that she shouldn't have, that standing up to him, no matter how weakly, never ended well these days. She felt the full force of his fist on her face before she even had a chance to put her hands up and defend herself. Dropping to the floor she instinctively curled into a ball, protecting herself from the inevitable barrage of hateful kicks that were now being aimed at her ribs and thighs. Julie knew better than to react, to make a noise even, clenching her teeth and listening to the voices to take her mind off the pain.

You deserve it, you deserve all of it.

You're lucky he's not left you, then where would you be?

You have failed as a wife, you couldn't even manage that!

Their words used to hurt her, but right now they were tame compared to Paul's cruel abuse. When the attack ended, Julie waited for a few minutes before she opening her eyes to see if he was still there. She couldn't see him but she stayed where she was a while longer, rigid inside and out, hoping that he had gone to bed and to sleep. In the beginning he would be remorseful, but not anymore, now he would just go to sleep as if nothing had happened. Slowly she sat up and leaned against the wall for a moment. She touched her face where his fist had been, she could feel that it was bruised, just like her ribs. She flinched as she heaved herself up, looking in the mirror at the angryred mark on her cheek and wondering if one day he would stop doing this, or if indeed he would do worse.

Julie took a deep breath and stood up straight, listening to what the voices were saying as they continued to mock her. They were right, telling her that she had nowhere to go, that she had got what she deserved. Paul often reminded her that if she left him she wouldn't get a penny of his money or anything from the house, that everything was in his name. The days of being in control of anything were long behind her, and she had long since given up even trying to get it back. Julie Margot was living the life that Julie Shuttleworth deserved, was born into, and she had been fooling herself to have ever thought she would have anything more.

She climbed the stairs on tiptoes, wanting to go and sleep in the spare room, but she had done that once before and it had angered him more. She slowly pushed open the bedroom door and was relieved to hear him snoring loudly, undressing quickly and climbing silently into the bed so as not to wake him, her heart racing as his breathing quietened and she felt his hand on her hip. She lay there without moving as he had sex with her; it was over in less than two minutes, before he rolled over and went back to sleep without saying a word. Julie closed her eyes, numb, wishing away the next few hours before she could legitimately leave him, if only for a few days while she was at work.

****

Julie looked in the rear-view mirror as the last of her tears fell from her chin. That was enough now, she told herself, she was allowed ten minutes to indulge in self-pity but now that time was up. She reached behind her and took her makeup bag out of the small case that was lying on the back seat, opening it in her lap. She took out her concealer and applied it liberally around her eye, blending it with her finger until the bruise and the dark circles were no longer visible, setting the creamy substance with powder. A slick of red lipstick, a burst of hairspray, and she emerged from her car as the person she wanted to be.

Julie walked briskly across the car park, trying to ignore the voices, today she didn't need their distraction. It was cold but she had forgotten her coat in her hurry to leave the house and she shivered as a plane roared above her as it came in to land. For four days she was going to live the part of her life that had actually gone according to her plan. She was going to go to Barbados and be Julie Margot, glamorous purser, and not Julie Margot, abused wife.

'Julie, oh my God, please tell me you're on the Barbados?!'

Julie left her thoughts and turned around to see who was so pleased to see her. Lisa stood there with a huge grin on her face which she instinctively mirrored.

'Yes, I am!' Julie felt an overwhelming gratitude to some unknown power for sending her a friend when she needed one. With so many crew at Osprey she only really made 'flight-friends', ones that were your best friend until you got in your car and drove home. A short nap later and she could barely remember where she had been, let alone their names. Lisa hugged her and Julie winced as she squeezed her bruised ribs, but she held in her cry. A memory slipped into her mind and immediately quashed her moment of happiness, remembering the last time she had seen Lisa and what she had said, the feeling of gratitude slipped away.

She's probably still sleeping with him, the voices tormented.

The bus arrived and they got on, stowing their bags in the rack and taking the only pair of seats available amongst the dozens of airport employees and other crew.

'So, what's new?' Lisa asked eagerly. 'We really must stay in contact more, Julie, you'll have to come and see me in Nottingham.'

'That would be lovely,' Julie agreed, knowing that it would never happen. 'What's new with you?' She sidestepped Lisa's question. One thing she knew about Lisa was that she loved to talk about herself, and that suited Julie, who would be avoiding talking about her own life as much as possible today.

'Oh babe, so much,' Lisa was beaming. 'How long since we saw each other last?'

'Eight years.' Julie didn't have to think too hard to work it out, remembering the day that her life had begun to slip out of her control like it was yesterday, how she had unwittingly ruined her life that day. Julie concentrated hard on not letting it show on her face.

'Well I'm married, and can you believe it, I have two children!'

Julie knew her face was showing her shock, and Lisa laughed at her.

'I know, who'd have thought I'd have settled down, hey, but when you find the right one you just know.'

'Congratulations,' Julie said with some effort. It wasn't fair, how she had everything, and didn't even know that she was partly responsible for the hell in which Julie lived now. 'How old are the children?' Julie pulled on her resources, the innate ability of crew to manufacture a conversation, and to smile with a look of genuine interest that isn't necessarily reflected on the inside.

'Evie is four and Jacob is two,' Lisa said, standing up as the bus pulled up outside the terminal building, flashing the screen-saver on her phone at her. Two beautiful children smiled at Julie, and she felt a stabbing pain in her heart. 'And the father is a six foot four sexy fireman.' She winked at Julie and turned to get her bag off the rack. Julie knew that her smile was no longer reaching her eyes. This was supposed to have been her, with everything, gloating, but Lisa had chipped away the first part of her dream that day eight years ago. She wrestled with the feeling of hatred that was brewing, she knew that she had no idea, perhaps she wouldn't have slept with Paul if he had mentioned Julie, but none of the attempts at reasoning made her feel any better and she just wanted to cry.

****

'Girls, the toilets are a mess, can someone please go and clean them up. They are supposed to be done every twenty minutes.' Julie was frustrated; why did she have to tell them all what to do, they knew their job so why weren't they doing it? The one with the blonde hair stood up, she didn't even know her name, or any of theirs, but she really didn't care today.

'I'll go,' she said. The others all stood up from where they had been sitting on the metal atlas boxes, picking them up and stowing them away without a word, avoiding looking at her.

116

'Can the rest of you please go and do juice and water, you are getting a break in crew rest so please keep busy while you are not on break.' She thought it was a fair enough comment, and it was her job as purser to supervise them after all, but she did prefer it when her crew just did what they were supposed to do without being told. Now no doubt they thought she was a bossy cow and she would probably find herself uninvited to their room party, but such was her role, she sighed.

Julie opened the duty-free bar and took out a bottle of gin, at least she could have her own party if necessary. She quickly put the bottle in her bag and closed the bar again, she cared so little about anything today that she wasn't even going to pay for it, to hell with everything.

You're a thief!

You're just trash, always were always will be!

Julie stopped, shocked for once by their words. Not so much by what they said, but by the truth in it. What was she thinking? Had she stooped so low, gone so far back to her roots? Even back then she had only stolen out of necessity, not because she was really a thief! No, she was better than that, wasn't she?

Julie opened a stowage and retrieved her purse from her bag, taking out the cash for her gin. Yes, Paul might have taken away her confidence and dreams, but she couldn't let him and the voices win completely, she still had her dignity, didn't she?

117

'How's things down here?' Lisa breezed into the galley with the smug smile on her face that had irritated Julie so much that she had opted to work in Economy, away from her.

'Good thanks, how's Business Class?'

'Demanding, and a bit precious.' She rolled her eyes.

'Oh dear, sometimes I prefer being in the galley back here than dealing with them these days,' Julie said. There was a time that she loved interacting with the passengers, but lately she didn't have the tolerance for them.

'Oh it's okay, since I've been part time they don't get to me like they used to.' She smiled as if she expected Julie to understand, which she didn't. 'Don't tell me you're still full time, hun?' Lisa's expression of shock and pity hit all the wrong places with Julie and she felt herself stand up straighter, she couldn't bear for anyone to feel sorry for her!

'Yes, for now, it's fine,' she said, hoping her smile was believable.

'But I thought you were marrying a lovely pilot? No children for you yet?'

'No, not yet.' Julie turned away from her and started to tidy the galley sides. She was relieved to hear the others come back and change the subject.

'Oh my God, I don't know how you kept a straight face,' the boy said as they both hunched over laughing.

'What happened?' Lisa asked.

'We were just by the toilets when a couple came out,' the girl explained.

'You should have seen their faces when they knew they'd been caught out,' he said. 'It was a picture.'

'And the best bit was when we got to the girl with juice and water and she's sitting with her friends, they aren't even travelling together!'

'She couldn't even look at us,' he said, and Julie could imagine the poor girl's embarrassment.

Julie looked at them all laughing, and wished she found it so funny, but she didn't; nothing seemed funny to her lately, just silly and unimportant. A call bell rang and she seized the opportunity to leave the galley before her lack of humour was too apparent.

'Yes, sir, can I help?' She looked down at the man who had called.

'Oh, sorry, I must have pressed it by accident,' he apologised. He had beautiful eyes that looked kind and made Julie smile back at him. 'But since you're here can I get a drink?' he grinned at her.

Once upon a time Julie would have flirted with him, especially when Paul was behaving badly, but for a long while now she had hidden away from any attention, it didn't make her feel better anymore.

'Certainly, what would you like?' Julie asked.

'A Jack Daniels and Coke please, and your number?' He was grinning at her and Julie returned it with her first genuine smile of the day, while rolling her eyes upward.

'One Jack Daniels and Coke coming up.' She reached up to cancel his call bell and walked back to the galley feeling much lighter than when she had left it; the attention had boosted her slightly.

'Yes, Paul Margot, you know the one, shags anything. No wonder she's a miserable cow.' Julie stopped at the galley entrance where they couldn't see her. So everyone knew that her husband slept around, and everyone thought she was a miserable cow, and now Lisa would know too that she had been the pathetic girlfriend of the pilot she had once slept with.

Julie turned and walked as quickly as she could to the front galley to get the drink. Her mind was racing. She couldn't even get away from it here, her life was terrible *everywhere*. She felt choked and was scared she might cry, seeking refuge in the toilet while she composed herself. Leaning on the edge of the washbasin, she looked at herself in the mirror. Was this to be her life now? Abused wife, disliked purser... victim?

Yes, a victim, that's what you are!

No! Julie stood back and took a deep breath. She felt angry and it somehow made her stronger. She could feel her whole body quiver as the anger grew until she stood defiantly looking at the person in front of her. She had spent years creating the person she had wanted to be, and she would not let one man take away everything she had worked for.

But you are weak now!

'SHUT UP!!' She screamed back at them in her head, they had too much to say lately and it was time they were quiet.

Passing Lisa on the way back to the galley she saw the awkwardness etched on her face as she kept her head down. Julie touched her arm to stop her, making her look up. 'It's okay,' she said. 'I know what my husband is.' She nodded once, her eyebrows raised in understanding, and gave her an accepting smile to say that it was all alright. The Julie that had emerged from the toilet was different to the one who had gone in. Things were going to change in her life… she didn't know how yet, but there wasn't a doubt in her mind that they were.

Chapter Twelve

Ditching + 20:00hrs

The fire was slowly burning out; the heat wasn't needed so much now that the sun was warming up the land. Alone outside for the first time Julie breathed in the crisp fresh air, finding something very calming about being cut off from the fast pace of the world she usually lived in. She looked up at the sun; from where it was directly above her she presumed it must be midday where they were now, and it seemed the others had been gone for a long time. She was so hungry, and knew that everyone else must be too.

'Alright, my gal?' Eric appeared behind her, stretching his arms out in front of him.

'Yes, thank you, Eric.' Julie smiled, she really was alright.

'Good, good. No sign of the others yet then?'

Julie shook her head slowly.

'My belly's rumbling,' Eric said, rubbing his ample stomach. 'I think I can go a while longer without starving though,' he laughed.

'I'm sure they'll be back soon,' Julie said kindly. 'Or we will have to go hunting Eric,' she teased.

'Well I'm up for that, used to go out with me dad when I was a kid. Don't suppose you've got an air rifle?'

'No, but she's got this.' Ken walked towards them and picked up the axe from the floor, with a smirk on his face that made Julie laugh.

'That'll do the job, bit brutal but if needs must,' Eric said seriously, taking the axe from Ken and waving it in the air, before laughing and handing it back to him. 'Thing is, love,' his voice lowered. 'The thing is, my Bet has a bit of diabetes and she needs to eat regular, nothing serious don't you worry, but if we don't get her something to eat soon enough she might not feel so good.'

'Oh, Eric, you should have said before, I'd have given her extra snacks.' Julie felt terrible, made worse by his humble approach.

'Oh no, there are people who need food more than us, can't have the kiddies going hungry.' He was smiling and Julie wanted to hug this lovely man. 'Just saying, in case you had a secret stash that was all.'

'I'll see what I can find.' She touched his arm and walked back to the tent. Inside she headed straight to the supplies area, and tried to ignore the hopeless feeling she got when she saw how little was left. A few bottles of water and a bag of pretzel packs. She took the pretzels and the water, suspecting Bet would also need to drink. There was quiet in the tent. She looked around at the groups, all just sat waiting to be rescued, probably presuming it would arrive at any time... but what if it didn't? Julie shook off that last thought, it didn't bear thinking about.

'Bet, I hear you might need something to eat.' Julie noticed how pale she looked, yet she still smiled sweetly back at her.

'I'm okay, love, let the children have them,' she said.

Julie knelt down so that she could talk to her quietly. 'Bet that is so lovely of you, and shows what a kind, selfless lady you are, but I have it on good authority that you need to eat something. I'm just sorry that this is all I have.' She put the pretzels down by her side with the water, standing up and addressing the rest of her group, who were all watching her.

'How is everyone else bearing up?' she asked.

'I've stayed in better hotels.' It was Eyecandy; she couldn't remember his real name, and realised she hadn't spoken to him since they were on the raft together. He looked different from yesterday, lack of sleep and grooming making him look much more 'average.' It crossed her mind

124

that he hadn't been outside with the men at all, that he was a different kind of man to them, still a boy in many ways.

'Haven't we all,' she agreed. 'Hang in there everyone, I'm sure they will be back with help soon.'

Julie turned away and took a moment to think. What if it wasn't just a few hours? Perhaps Bet wasn't the only one who needed food for medical reasons, and there were only a few bottles of water left. She inhaled – there was no point in hanging around worrying, it was time to start doing.

'I'm sorry, I forgot your name?' She turned and addressed Eyecandy.

'Craig,' he replied.

'Craig, how do you fancy going and looking for a river or a source of water?' she asked.

'Erm, is it safe?' He looked reluctant. Julie tried to understand him and not judge, he had obviously never been a Boy Scout, and had probably had a very sheltered upbringing before finding fame. Now though, being famous wasn't any help to anyone.

'I won't send you on your own, but we need to try and find some food and water, just in case they are much longer.' She was being firmer now, there was no point in sitting around waiting like this, people needed to be kept busy.

Julie gathered the crew together, taking charge of the situation.

125

'Okay, we need to find water, and food, in case help doesn't come soon. Gather up any empty bottles you have to collect it in. The fresher the water the better, but we do have some purification tablets in the survival kits. Laurence, I want you to take my man Craig, and one other with you.' Laurence nodded. 'Antonio, pick two people to go with you, anyone with military training or knowledge of the outdoors would be best.'

'Yes, boss,' Antonio said sincerely, nodding his head once.

'You girls, I need you to check on every person individually, find out if they have any medical conditions and so on, they might not want to tell you unless you ask,' she said, thinking of Bet. 'We don't want anyone to get sick for the sake of prioritising them for food and water.' The girls nodded. 'I'm going to take a walk back to the lake, see if the boats are still there, and make sure they are visible to any planes.'

She was thinking on her feet, but as she spoke she could see everyone sitting up to listen. They needed a plan, and someone to follow, and she was finally that person, now that Iain had gone. 'Now, check your watches.'

Julie was glad that they all had to wear watches as part of their uniform. 'I make it 1725, that's London time. Don't go too far, and meet back here at 2200, boys. I will set a flare off at 2200 if any of you aren't back, in case you get lost, look out for that.' She presumed they were four or five hours behind, so that would have everyone safely back before dark, and give her time to get to the lake and back. 'Actually, boys, why don't you take a set of mini flares with you, just in case you need any help getting back.' The boys nodded. The mini flares, eight in a pack, would make sure they could be located, and Julie was impressed at how many things from the survival kit were actually coming in useful so far.

She was pleased to see everyone was nodding in agreement with her plans. 'Right, let's get going and do what we need to do,' she said with gusto, like they were going to war, or on a flight to Jamaica.

****

'Ken, would you mind coming with me back to the lake? I just want to make sure the rafts are still visible,' Julie asked, catching him just outside the tent with Milton.

'Good call, no problem.' Ken smiled.

'Milton, are you okay to wait here and keep an eye on things?' Milton mock-saluted her. She was increasingly grateful that these two dependable and reliable men had ended up in her raft yesterday. 'Now we just need a third person,' she mused, walking back into the tent and looking around. 'Cheryl, would you mind coming with me and Ken down to the lake, we need a third person?'

Cheryl looked up from where she was sitting with Phil. 'Erm,' she said and turned to look at him.

'I'll come, I'll be more use to you.' Phil flashed his fake smile and started to get up.

'Thank you for your kind offer, Phil,' Julie smiled back with as much fakeness as he had, 'but I was hoping you would stay here. I've asked the girls to identify anyone with medical conditions that may need attention, and as our resident doctor, it would be good if you could assess their needs if they have any.' Julie knew that flattery was the only way to talk to big egos.

'Well, okay, that sounds sensible.' He puffed out his chest. 'Don't you go holding them back though, Cheryl,' he said in a condescending tone to his wife. Julie felt the hairs on the back of her neck stand up in indignation on Cheryl's behalf, but Cheryl didn't even seem to notice.

'I think that means you are allowed to come with me, Cheryl.' Julie held her hand out and helped her up.

'Thank you,' Cheryl said as soon as they were out of earshot. Julie just gave her a knowing smile in return.

'Right, Ken, Cheryl, let's get going,' she said, leading them in the direction from where they had come just the day before.

It was a beautiful day, the sun was shining in the clear blue sky, and the temperature was perfect. Julie was glad it wasn't too hot or too cold as she had struggled with both of the extremes lately. They walked in silence for a while, Julie moving aside to let Ken lead the way since he was the most confident and able of the three. It crossed her mind that it might have been more sensible to have selected another man, in case they needed strength, but when she looked at Cheryl she knew that she was strong, in fact she looked stronger now than she had earlier; something had changed in her since they spoke and Julie was pleased to see it. As they passed another of the life jackets that she had tied around a tree, Julie's thoughts slipped back to the raft, and then to the plane. She began to feel fearful, residual shock over what had happened bubbling up inside, and the feelings threatened to take a hold of her.

'So, tell us about yourself, Ken,' she blurted out. The silence had been peaceful up until now, but it was leaving space for bad thoughts, and she needed to distract herself.

'What do you want to know?' He glanced over his shoulder with an amused look on his face. Julie knew some men weren't good at small talk, and that she was probably going to need to draw it out of him.

'Well let's start with where you come from and your age,' she began.

'I grew up all over, my father was in the military so we moved every couple of years. Now I live in St Albans. As for my age, I'll be fifty-three tomorrow.'

'Oh wow, well I do hope you don't have to spend your birthday out here, I'm so sorry,' Julie apologised, there was certainly nowhere to organise a birthday cake or bubbles where they were.

'I think I wouldn't mind that, I love the outdoors,' Ken said. At no point had he seemed the slightest bit fazed by their situation, and Julie thought he could probably survive out here alone for a very long time. Unlike her and most of the others, he didn't need the protection of the group, but she was glad that he was with them. Julie listened to the noises around them and noticed that the sounds of the animals didn't make her jump anymore, in fact their calls had become part of the quiet. She had always believed that she didn't like the outdoors, but in truth she had never been camping, or walked in a forest before now – perhaps it was something she would try to do more when she got home.

'Wife and children?' Julie asked.

'Ex-wife, two children, Beth and Trey, both live nearby with their mum, twenty-one and twenty-three.'

'Girlfriend?'

'No.' Ken was laughing. 'Shoe size eleven, I play rugby, like a drink down the local, am retired from the military but still work for them in an advisory role. Anything I missed?'

Cheryl laughed now, and Julie felt embarrassed. 'I'm sorry, I can't help being nosy,' she apologised. It was true, most crew were so open about everything, you would learn every detail of their lives in the galley over a cup of tea at 3am, that she forgot *normal* people weren't used to divulging so much about themselves to someone they had only just met.

'It's fine, nothing to hide here,' he said, stopping until she was beside him before carrying on walking alongside her.

'And what about you, now that you know everything about me?' he asked. Julie looked and met his eyes. She noticed the dark brown ring that encircled the bright blue for the first time, and was captivated for a moment. He was smiling at her, and the skin creased down the side of his face, down to the strong jaw that encompassed the smile, that formed around the perfectly imperfect teeth... Julie realised she was staring and looked quickly at the floor. Ken was far from her normal 'type', she preferred them younger, but with the younger ones insecurities had crept in as she had started to acknowledge her age, and so lately she had lost her usual drive.

'Oh, married, divorced, no kids, and no cat.' She was relieved to make the other two laugh.

'That's a shame, you'd make a lovely wife, you are very kind,' Cheryl said behind them. Julie took a moment to process the last bit; it wasn't a compliment she had received much before, but she liked it. Life had taken her on many paths, ones where she had to be strong, sexy, clever, resilient, a leader, a nurse, but this was a new one, having to look after these people, and she liked the warm feeling that it gifted her.

'Thank you, Cheryl,' she said humbly.

'Did you bring the gin?' Cheryl asked with a smirk.

Ken turned around and raised an eyebrow at Julie, who put a finger to her lips and shushed her confidant.

Finally, the trees began to clear and the ground began to get softer; Julie had forgotten about the boggy ground that had forced them inland. As the water opened up in front of them she thought they must have come out at a different place. The view looked the same, but the rafts were gone and so were the life jackets that Antonio had left to show their direction.

'So that's why they can't find us,' Ken said thoughtfully, his hands on his hips, looking up and down the coast.

'Where did the boats go?' asked Cheryl, looking at him for the answer.

'The tide must have taken them,' he said without turning around.

'Do lakes have tides?' Cheryl asked. Julie was thinking the same thing.

'It's a bay, not a lake, unfortunately, and this bay certainly does,' Ken said gravely.

'So wherever they have ended up, they could possibly be looking for us miles away?' Cheryl said, a tinge of hopelessness in her voice.

'Yes, but they should take the tides into consideration eventually,' Julie said, recalling something from her training and feeling calmer than she would have thought she should.

She looked out to the middle of the bay and remembered how the plane had floated there so magically only the day before.

'Yes, they will, but it might be a day or two. Maybe we should try and catch some fish while we are here.'

'Sorry?!' Julie laughed – that wasn't in her manual.

'I'm serious, ladies, I'm going to teach you how to fish,' he said decisively. 'This trip won't be in vain, we are going to get back to camp with dinner.'

Julie grimaced, suddenly she was in an episode of that awful survival show, she hadn't expected things to get this desperate!

Ten minutes later they each had a 'spear' that Ken had carved for them out of thin branches using a piece of sharp stone, and were standing a few feet away from each other digging it aimlessly into the shallow water. Julie felt ridiculous at first, wondering how on earth she had ended up in this scenario and if she was going to wake up soon.

'I got one,' Cheryl shrieked, holding up her pole. A silver fish flapped around frantically on the end of it and Julie felt terrible for it suffering so that they could eat. It only lasted a moment though, before Ken had released it and put it out of its misery by hitting it over the head with a rock. Julie's stomach flipped, she wasn't made for such things, but she watched Cheryl pick up her catch proudly, with a big smile on her face.

'Well done, Cheryl,' Julie congratulated her, it was good to see her realising her abilities, even if it was for something so obscure and unnecessary in the civilised world.

In the next hour the others caught fish after fish as Julie watched, unable to catch anything other than leaves and plants. Perhaps she could have tried harder, concentrated more, but deep down her heart just wasn't in it.

'We had best get back,' she said eventually, looking at her watch and seeing the time.

Ken looked over at her, a pile of fish at his feet. 'Well at least our trip wasn't wasted.'

'Yes, sorry, I don't think there are any fish over here,' Julie apologised.

'That's okay, since me and Cheryl caught them all, you can carry them back,' he said.

Julie opened her eyes wide as she thought through that scenario. It was bad enough that she had been wearing her uniform for nearly two whole days now, but despite a decompression, a ditching, and camping, she had managed to keep it clean so far, and didn't think that she smelt. Now this man, who up until now she had liked, was suggesting she walk all the way back with armfuls of wet, slippery, smelly fish, that would leave her absolutely filthy, and worse still stinking of fish! No, her imagination was going wild, how would she explain to the rescue services why she smelt so bad when they found them?

The sound of hysterical laughing snapped her back into the moment and she looked up to see the others pink-faced and both holding their stomachs, they were laughing so hard.

'Your face,' gasped Ken, struggling to breathe.

Julie was so relieved to see he had been joking she didn't mind that they were laughing at her expense. 'Oh thank God,' she said, 'I really thought you meant it.'

'You could see that by the look on your face,' laughed Cheryl.

Julie was puzzled though, since she wasn't the solution to an apparent problem. 'So, how are we going to get them back?'

'Like this,' Ken said, proceeding to skewer them onto his spear in one big fish kebab.

Julie nodded, impressed, especially when Cheryl took his lead and did the same with her haul.

'Now we just need one on each end, I'll go at the back and you two take turns at the front. There's a lot of fish here, it will get heavy.'

And just like that they walked back to camp with over thirty fish for dinner, and a new page for the survival manual... Julie made a mental note to have it added when she got back to the office!

Chapter Thirteen

18 years earlier

Julie saw the girl's face drop as she realised who she was, it was the same way that Paul's had dropped when she had told him this morning that she was on his flight today. That was all the proof she had needed that he was screwing someone on the crew, and that her efforts to swap onto the flight had paid off. Since arriving at check-in she had been sitting alone in the briefing room looking at the names on her crew list as they came in to select their working positions, wondering which of them it was, but now she knew.

'I'm going to put the positions down today, you are working up the front with me,' she smiled and wrote a position number next to her name. She saw the girl's lip quiver as she tried to smile back, and for a second she felt sorry for her, but only for a second. 'I don't think we have met before, I'm Julie Margot.' She extended her hand and took the limp one that was offered back. 'Flight manager. The captain, Paul Margot, is my husband.'

Julie had worked hard to get her promotion six months ago, it was good to be the boss, to do things the way you wanted to, to be in control.

'Nice to meet you, Julie,' said the girl whose name according to the list was Hannah. 'I thought Harry Moult was the manager today?'

'Yes, he was, but I swapped with him last night so that I could fly with my husband, have a nice night away together.' Julie was enjoying watching her awkwardness. Maybe it was a little calculated that she had hidden Paul's phone, but she hadn't wanted him to warn her. She wanted the satisfaction of watching them both squirm, it was the least she deserved. 'I've packed some nice new underwear,' she winked, with an exaggerated grin, 'and of course we will all be going out for dinner tonight, won't we?'

Hannah nodded. It was Cape Town, and everyone went out for steak and wine in Cape Town.

'Have you brought anyone with you?' Julie could see that Hannah was desperate to get out of the room, but she couldn't resist digging. Hannah shook her head. 'Have you left your husband at home?'

'Yes, he has to work,' Hannah mumbled, turning towards the door. There it was, she was married too. They were both having an affair, her husband and Hannah. It hadn't been lost on Julie that despite seeming to hate her sometimes, Paul didn't leave her. He still wanted the comforts of a wife who did everything for him, that went out with him, looked after him, and kept up his image of a good man and good husband, and if Hannah was married too he hadn't been put under any pressure to leave her. Julie watched the somewhat plain girl, who was so opposite to her with her dark hair and curvy figure, leave the room and wondered what he got out of it, why he needed more when she would have given him everything.

Things had somewhat improved at home, a bad routine medical check had scared him into cutting down on the drinking and so the outbursts had whittled away, and on most days he was quite tolerable. With Julie it was always about having a plan though, and for a while there she had been lost, but not now. The way things were at present would perhaps have been enough for her once, even knowing that he was having an affair, but he had killed something in her that she couldn't get back, the dream was over for Julie and she was on to the next one.

Paul walked past the window of the briefing room just as Hannah walked out. She watched their awkward exchange of looks before they both put their heads down and scurried away in different directions. Julie smiled; she was going to enjoy this trip.

****

'Gentlemen, we are just about to go out with the dinner service, would you like anything to drink before we get busy?' Julie asked as she entered the flight deck and closed the door behind her. If she didn't ask now you could guarantee all pilots would wait until you were at your busiest before asking for a cappuccino or something equally as awkward.

'No thank you.' Paul barely turned around from his left-hand seat. The first officer, Neil, smiled broadly at her, compensating for her husband's indifference.

'No thank you, Julie, how are things in the cabin?'

'All good,' she replied cheerfully. 'I'm having a bit of trouble with one of the girls, she's clearly got a lot on her mind and is a bit hopeless.'

'Oh dear,' Neil said sympathetically.

'It's fine, we all have our off days,' Julie sighed. 'I'll have a chat with poor Hannah later, see if I can find out what's going on. It's probably man trouble.' Julie rolled her eyes and smiled, turning from Neil to Paul, who had twisted his neck slightly. Despite not looking at her, she knew he was listening. She left the flight deck satisfied. Paul was brazen enough not to be squirming now as others might, but he wasn't completely devoid of feelings, and the one thing she knew he hated most was humiliation. Hopefully he was suitably worried now.

'I'll lay up this side with you,' Julie said to Hannah, who had so far struggled to make eye contact with her. She was confident that Sam, who was working in the galley, was aware of the situation, going by the looks that were exchanged between them every time Julie was around. Julie wasn't going to feel awkward though, that wasn't her place today.

'Okay.' Hannah got on one end of the trolley and they wheeled it through into Business Class.

'Any wine for you, Mr Humphrey?' Julie asked the small weaselly man in 1A. He was one of their top flyers, with a reputation that preceded him, but he liked Julie, she knew how to handle him. 'I know you like a French wine so I can recommend this.' She held out a bottle for him to see.

'Well remembered,' he said, impressed. 'That will be fine, thank you.'

'Would you like to try it first?'

He nodded and Julie poured a small amount into his glass, watching as he swilled it around, first in his glass and then in his peculiarly small mouth.

'Are you out on business again?' Julie asked as she poured some more into his glass.

'Yes, and then I'm going to take advantage and stay for a few days in Camps Bay.'

'Oh how lovely, is anyone joining you?'

'Are you available?' He gave her a smile that belonged on a creepy movie villain.

'Well that's a tempting offer,' *if you were a foot taller with a bit more hair, better teeth, worked out occasionally...*she added silently.

'I have a villa with an infinity pool, a butler and a fridge full of Dom Pérignon,' he said persuasively. Julie ached to be there, just not with him, no amount of expensive champagne would be enough.

'It sounds wonderful, it's a shame I have work,' she said. 'Thank you for the lovely offer though, I must get on,' and she pushed the trolley forward to catch up with Hannah who had served three people in the time she had served one.

'Don't tell my husband, but I think I may have just got a better offer,' Julie said in a hushed tone across the trolley. 'These captains aren't what they used to be, especially my husband, and Mr Humphrey has more than enough money to make up for his lack of looks.'

Hannah's eyes met hers for the first time, and Julie could tell she was trying to work out whether she was joking or not. She looked down at the trolley and took the things she needed from it, turning to lay up the lady in 3D, supressing the smile that was trying to break at the corners of her mouth.

Back in the galley Julie took a piece of paper and rested it on the galley side so that everyone could see her writing on it.

Dear Mr Humphrey

Thank you for your offer, I would love to join you.

Call me tomorrow

Julie

She then added a phone number, not hers, and folded the paper in two. She looked up quickly, catching Hannah averting her eyes, and wondered how long it would take to get to Paul. When Hannah had left the galley and Sam was looking the other way, Julie threw the paper into the bin, as she had never had any intention of giving it to him. On another piece of paper she wrote her name and her real number, walking confidently down the aisle until she reached 8A. The beautiful South African rugby-player-type that was sitting there had been flirting with her earlier, and he didn't need a fridge full of Dom Pérignon to tempt her.

'Call me when you are next in London,' Julie said, putting the folded note down on his table.

'I certainly will,' he said with the sexiest smile she had seen in a long time. By the time he came back to London she would be available for him.

****

Julie could tell that Paul was fuming, the tension had been radiating from him since they landed. She hadn't seen him and Hannah talking, but she knew that they had, and that he was struggling with his hypocritical jealousy. She was loving acting so innocent, sitting next to him on the bus to the hotel as if they were a happy couple, and chatting to the others around them, forcing him to join in.

In the hotel lobby they lined up to sign in and take their keys. Julie knew that Paul was saving up his outburst until they were alone in their room, but she had already thought about this.

'Darling, I think we should have a date night, I'm going to go and get ready in my own room,' she said as she signed the sheet.

'Romantic,' said Neil, overhearing her.

Julie smiled and kissed her husband's cold cheek, which was turning very pink. She laughed inside at Paul's struggle to keep his composure. Looking down the list of names she said loudly, 'Hannah, I'm next door to you, knock for me when you are ready to come down for dinner.' She couldn't have planned it better, it was as if a higher being had organised the allocation of rooms. Now Paul couldn't knock on her door, or Hannah's, without the other hearing. Hannah looked over at her with a small, obviously forced smile, dismay in her eyes. Paul was almost crimson as she blew him a kiss and strutted to the lifts, wheeling her case behind her, wearing the biggest, most authentic grin on her face.

****

They sat on the terrace outside of the restaurant on the waterfront. The buildings around reflected in the water that had turned ink-dark as the sun set. The colonial-style restaurants were lit up and each one was packed full of people sitting inside and out, enjoying the food and the atmosphere in one of South Africa's finest settings. Julie sipped the cold white wine and ignored the looks of hatred from Paul, whom she had managed to seat herself further down the table from. So far there had been safety in numbers but she knew he was waiting for his chance to show her how angry he was… so she smiled wider, laughed louder, and enjoyed her moment.

'Waiter, can we get some more wine, please?' she called to the boy who had been serving them. The starters were still arriving but the wine had already run out, it was a crew after her own heart.

'Maybe you should slow down a bit,' Paul said. The crew who were sitting between them all looked down at their food, privy to the cracks in their relationship. Julie looked at Paul and smiled, amused by the way his face was an open book, telling the story of his inward struggle.

'Oh don't be such a bore, Paul,' she said, raising her now full glass at him. 'Don't you think he's boring, girls?'

She asked the question to Hannah and Sam, who up until now had been huddled together, one obviously needing the other's support. They both gave a pathetic smile back that just spurred Julie on. She turned in her seat to face the other end of the table, the end that weren't yet subdued by the atmosphere between her and Paul, and joined their much more upbeat dialogue.

The main course arrived, a sea of steaks and creamed spinach, while Julie had opted for the kingklip and lobster. She loved fish but Paul despised it so much that she never cooked it at home, or ate it when she was going to be close to him; since neither applied tonight she hoped that he had noticed her menu choice.

'How is your steak, darling?' she asked him, just for fun, to see how he would react. He nodded, she could tell he was struggling to eat whilst his stomach was in knots. 'This fish is amazing,' she said with a smile and held her glass up to him again, taking a big sip before filling it back up. The redness of his neck that showed his inward battle satisfied Julie and she went back to talking to Neil, who was much more fun.

As the main course plates were cleared away Julie turned around to see Paul standing up and walking over towards her. She felt a knot underneath her ribs and hoped that it didn't show, forcing her smile to go higher.

'Let's go back to the hotel, Julie,' he said in a controlled tone, taking some notes from his pocket and giving them to Neil. 'That should cover ours.'

'Oh, no, I'm not ready to go back yet, Paul. I'll see you later,' she said and turned her back on him.

'Julie, we are going, *now,*' he said, his voice was shaking.

'No, Paul, I'm sorry but you will have to go without me. I'm enjoying myself.' Julie took another sip of wine, for courage. 'We are going for a dance after this,' she said, looking at the others for affirmation.

'Yes, we were just saying about going to The Hard Rock,' said Neil, with a slight slur. Julie was relieved that he was so unaware of the dangerous territory they were in.

'I think my wife has had enough.' Paul had put his hand under her arm and was actually trying to pick her up.

'Paul, please let go of me,' Julie said firmly. She knew he hated a scene, and she needed him to know that if he carried on there would be one. He let go of her and took a step back; she could tell that he didn't know what to do in this unprecedented situation. Julie stood up slowly. In contrast to her husband she felt strangely calm and in control.

'Neil, don't go without me,' she said, putting her napkin down on the table. 'I just need to talk to my husband.'

Julie walked to the water's edge, leaning over the barrier and taking a deep breath before turning to face him. He was opening his mouth to say something and she raised her hand sharply to stop him.

'Paul, why don't you take your little slapper back to your room, because I am not leaving this restaurant with you.'

Paul stared at her.

'Surely you don't think I didn't know about Hannah?!'

'Oh, that's rich, coming from the person who slipped a passenger her phone number,' Paul spat, clutching at straws.

Julie threw her head back and laughed. 'That was fake, I just did it to see if the little cow told you!' She looked over at Hannah, and was surprised that she didn't even hate her, her marriage was broken a long time before she had come along.

'When we get back you will hear from my solicitor, I've filed for divorce.'

Now Paul laughed, but it was weak. 'What the hell are you going to do without me? You don't have anything,' he mocked.

'Oh, but my solicitor says I will be entitled to plenty, Paul, so I will be absolutely fine.' She didn't add that she had taken lots of advice, and that there was no way that she would be leaving their marriage with nothing, not by a long way. Nor did she add that she had already rented a room, that there was no way she would be getting in a car with him and going home when they got back to Heathrow, that she had been secretly packing up her things and moving them out this past week. Nor did she say that she had evidence of his cheating so that he couldn't contest the divorce. No matter what she might have done in retaliation years ago, nobody knew, and for the purpose of getting as much as she could from him, she was squeaky clean and very much the victim. He could find all of that out when they got back.

'You'll get nothing, I promise you.' He said it with such certainty, confirming her suspicions that he had hidden his money, but she was prepared for that.

'Paul, I have medical records as long as my arm of injuries you have caused me back when you thought it was okay to use me as a punchbag. Now if you don't want them finding their way out to the world, I would suggest you play nicely.'

Paul was speechless, his mouth opening and shutting like a goldfish in a bowl. Julie hadn't really been to a doctor, but she was glad to see that he believed she might just have. They both knew that if it got out, and worse still if she really had the evidence to prosecute him, it could ruin his precious career. There was fear in his eyes as he stood frozen to the spot and processed her threat.

'Now, my love, why don't you just fuck off as far as you can, and when you get there fuck off a little further… you're ditched,' she said, revelling in her rare use of such foul language, and walking back to the table with a huge, liberated smile on her face.

Chapter Fourteen

Ditching + 24:30hrs

The reaction was mixed as they walked back into the camp, from applause to bewilderment, to disappointment that they had come back with fish and not a rescue party. People began to spill out of the tent, just as Antonio appeared from the trees on the other side with his group, each carrying several full bottles of water.

'We found a river, boss, not far from here,' he said, the three of them putting the bottles down on the ground. 'Feesh,' he said in his Italian drawl, nodding to show he was impressed. 'Shame there is no chips huh?'

'Yes, a crying shame,' Ken agreed. Milton had relieved Julie and Cheryl of their end of the burden and the two men were now laying their catch out on a bed of leaves that had been hurriedly made.

'And the boats, are they still there?' Antonio asked.

Julie shook her head, standing with her hands on her hips. 'No, I'm afraid not, it seems the tide took everything, and that is why they haven't found us.'

'Surely they could find us with the radio beacon?' he asked.

Julie looked around; she had forgotten about that until now. 'I have no idea what the captain did with it, I haven't seen it since he was switching it on when we first arrived,' she said thoughtfully. It crossed her mind that he might not have managed to turn it on at all, she had never checked, or that he might even have taken it with him.

Antonio shook his head, cursing in Italian. 'So, we should put something up high, no?' He looked up at the trees that loomed overhead and all around them.

'Good thinking.' Ken turned around from where he and Milton were gutting the fish with sharp stones that he had brought back from the water.

'We'll need to get the fire going properly again too,' Milton said.

'The smokier the better,' added Julie.

A moment later Antonio reappeared looking somewhat ridiculous, wearing several deflated life jackets one over the other. 'I will be back soon,' he said, marching to the nearest tree and launching himself up it. Julie watched in mixed amusement and horror as he climbed with the agility of a child, panicking that he would fall out at any moment, until he was so high that she couldn't watch any more.

The girls had appeared beside her, waiting for an update, and Julie briefed them on the situation.

'Nadine, could you locate the water purification tablets and try to make this water drinkable?' She looked at her watch, it was almost ten o'clock, Laurence should be back soon. 'Let's arrange a briefing at half past ten, get everyone together and I'll update them all.'

Julie looked up and quickly wished that she hadn't, the thin branches of the tree waving as Antonio climbed amongst them. A flash of colour moved upwards, landing somewhere on the top, followed by another, and another, until from the ground the tree looked like it had yellow and orange leaves. She hoped from the air it would look more obviously like a signal. No one spoke as the hero of the moment descended, Julie running through what she knew about treating broken bones in her mind. As he appeared beneath the branches and dropped the last few feet onto the ground she exhaled and felt her shoulders relax.

'Well done, Antonio,' she said, relieved that he had got down in one piece. Her feeling of relief was quickly replaced though, her heart skipping a beat as a loud noise made everyone turn and look upwards.

'Sheet,' remarked Antonio, as they watched the flare shoot through the sky.

'We will go.' Ken was by her side with Milton, both looking in the direction of where it had come from. Julie's mind raced through all of the reasons why Laurence would have set it off, hoping that the simplest one, that they were lost, was the right one.

'I will come with you.' Antonio followed them into the trees and Julie watched on as they disappeared. She looked around, all of her heroes were gone now, and she felt vulnerable in their absence. She walked into the tent, casting her eye over the people left there, looking for anyone who looked like they could light a fire, cook dinner, fight off bears...

'Everything okay, love?' Eric asked, walking over to her.

'I hope so, Eric, some of the group have got lost, that's all. Hopefully the captain will be back with help soon,' she smiled. 'I don't suppose you know much about bonfires?'

'Course I do,' he winked. 'I was a right scallywag growing up,' he winked again.

'That's great.' Julie was relieved. 'Well there is one that needs attention outside if you don't mind?'

'My pleasure.' He signalled to Bet, who got up and followed him outside. Julie noticed how pale she still was, and hoped that the fish would go some way to making her feel a little better.

She walked over to her girls, who looked like they were carrying out a science experiment, all huddled on the floor around the bottles of water, dropping tablets into them. 'I'm really hoping help comes before we actually have to drink this,' Jody said with a frown, holding up a bottle and examining the murky water.

'I'm hoping it arrives before this number two does,' Nadine said, and started giggling, making Julie and the others laugh. She hadn't given much thought to such things, leaving each individual to worry about their most personal needs.

'Carry on there, girls, I'll speak to everyone in small groups.' She didn't fancy having to gather them all together again, with all the focus on her and without the back up of her heroes. She walked from one group to the next, checking on their welfare and updating them with her small offering of information. She estimated the time was about five o'clock now, a few hours of daylight left before they would have to face up to another night out here.

'Anything we can do?' A young man of maybe just twenty years old offered. He was sitting next to a man who was an older version of him, his father, Julie presumed.

'Well we need wood for the fire, if you could gather some up?'

Both men jumped up. 'No problem, glad to have something useful to do, sitting around here is sending me crazy,' the older of the two said, holding out his hand to Julie. 'Max, and this is my son Jake, and my wife Sandra.' His petite wife stood up and offered her hand too.

'Very pleased to meet you all.' Julie shook their hands, glad to have found some more able people, that things would still get done in the absence of those she had become so reliant on.

'No sign of a rescue party yet then?' Sandra asked.

'I'm afraid not, but I'm sure they will find us soon,' Julie said, trying her best to be reassuring.

A baby crying caught her attention, and she walked back over to where Chloe was sitting trying to comfort little Reuben.

'I don't think I have enough milk for him,' she said quietly, with a helpless look on her face.

Julie took him from her, noting that he was now nappy free, and a potential hazard to her clean uniform. She absorbed the warmth of his body regardless, and lost herself for a moment in his eyes as he stopped crying and stared back at her.

'Now that's better,' she cooed. 'We are going to feed Mummy up so that she can feed you,' she said, smiling down at his quizzical face for a while before handing the now contented bundle back to his parents.

'He really loves you,' Chloe said, making Julie smile. As much as she knew it wasn't a good idea, she thought a lot of the little guy too.

'Julie, I'm hungry,' Ruby said and Julie turned to see the little girl standing behind her with a sad look on her face.

'Well we have some fish for dinner, and before we know it we will be out of here,' she said with as much brightness as she could muster.

'I don't like fish,' she said, and Julie thought she might cry. She remembered when she was about Ruby's age, and how her mum had smacked her for being fussy, in the days before she gave up cooking for her altogether.

'Well then, let's play make believe, if you could have anything you wanted to eat right now, what would you have?' Julie asked. If she had been lucky enough to have children she would never have forced them to eat things they didn't like, in fact there were a lot of things she would never have done the way her own mother had.

'Chicken nuggets,' Ruby grinned and Julie laughed.

'Well, here you go, six chicken nuggets, would you like fries?' Julie pretended to hand her the imaginary order, Ruby chuckled and nodded her head. 'Here you go, one large fries.' Julie handed her more imaginary food.

'Thank you,' said Ruby, pretending to eat the gourmet dinner.

'You are very welcome,' Julie said. 'I am sure the minute we get out of here Mummy will take you for chicken nuggets.' She wished so badly that she could magic some up right now for the little girl who was being so brave. 'We are all hungry, darling, but I promise you we will get out of here soon.' The little girl wrapped her arms around Julie's waist and Julie bent down to hug her back. She was aware that she had just made a promise, and that you should never break promises, and she squeezed Ruby a little tighter as she visualised her eating those chicken nuggets.

There was a commotion outside and Julie patted Ruby on the shoulder, sending her back to her mum. She moved quickly out of the tent, and turned to look in the same direction as everyone else was. From the trees emerged the men, headed by Ken. His face looked worried, and Julie's stomach sank.

Chapter Fifteen

13 years earlier

Julie poured herself a glass of champagne and sat on her balcony overlooking the park. She smiled as she took a sip, the bubbles dancing down her throat.

'Happy birthday, Julie,' she said as she raised her glass to herself, closing her eyes and feeling the sunshine on her skin. She was forty today, a number that both terrified and exhilarated her at the same time. She was terrified that she was heading towards an age where she would become invisible, and exhilarated by where she was now that she had reached it. She turned and looked over her shoulder into her living room, with its high ceilings and expensive furnishings. The chandelier that hung sparkling in the middle of the room had cost half of her year's salary, but she had done extremely well out of her divorce and could afford it. Now, she sat as the owner of a beautiful apartment in central London and she was happy with where she was. Better still, her lawyer had secured her a regular payment from Paul that would keep her in this lifestyle… life was good.

She took another sip and allowed herself to remember the systematic abuse that she had been through, because she could see now that that was what it had been. A small smile formed on her lips; these memories weren't painful, because each insult, each punch, each kick, had been converted into money, she deserved every single penny of her settlement, she had earned it.

Julie stood up as the buzzer rang on her intercom, looking at her reflection in the long, gilded mirror that stood leant against the wall. The silk lining of the pewter wrap dress skimmed her slim body, the chiffon top layer catching shadows as it moved with her. Her hair, recently highlighted, was set in a big chignon, held with a hundred pins by the hairdresser, she had treated herself for her birthday. She quickly applied a layer of red lip gloss before turning her designer heels towards the hall and letting her visitor in.

'Wow, you look stunning,' said George, affirming what she had already seen, stepping through the front door.

'Thank you very much,' she said. He leaned in to kiss her and she allowed him the smallest peck, protecting her lip gloss. 'I'll just get my coat.' Julie walked to her dressing room and picked out her long red dress coat; it was late April and there was still a chill in the evening air. She looked at the handbags displayed on shelves above her shoes, and picked the small black Chanel one, a classic, and not a Chinese fake like other crew proudly sported. In some people's apartments this might have been a spare bedroom, but she had no need for one of those, and she had put it to much better use anyway.

'Okay, I'm ready,' she said. George was standing with his hands in his pockets looking down at his shoes. His floppy dark blonde hair fell forward, before being pushed back high on his head when he looked up.

'I brought you a present,' he said, taking a small package wrapped in blue tissue paper from the inside pocket of his suit jacket. Julie took it from him; it really hadn't occurred to her that he would buy her a gift, he didn't need to abide by those sorts of rules, their relationship wasn't like that. She opened the wrapper carefully, revealing the small box inside. Opening it, she smiled at the beautiful bracelet that sparkled back at her – she knew diamonds when she saw them.

'You shouldn't have,' she said, looking up at her handsome date.

'I couldn't not get you a present for your birthday,' he grinned and took it from her, proceeding to put it on her wrist.

If only he knew it was her fortieth, she thought, would she have got a bigger present? No, he probably wouldn't be here. Despite what some would have classed as a hard life so far, Julie had managed to look younger than her years. As far as George was concerned she was only thirty-three, just three years older than him.

'Do you like it?' he asked.

She twisted her wrist to let the diamonds catch the light. 'I love it,' she said, kissing him properly this time.

'I've booked us a table at the Ritz,' he said as they walked out of the building and into a waiting car. Julie thought how lucky she was, to go to the Ritz on her birthday, to be spoiled by this handsome young man who couldn't hurt her. Everything was good about this relationship, Julie had learned from Paul never to depend on a man again, to live in the moment and write her own story. So far things were working out well for her.

The car stopped and the driver got out to open the door for them both. 'Thank you, Michael, I'll call you when we're done,' George said. Julie took a deep breath as she stood up, aware of her posture and to make sure she was smiling, as the flashes began.

'George, over here,' they called. The paparazzi seemed to be everywhere if you were on the arm of a famous actor. This was the third time they had been out on a date since they met on a flight from Los Angeles two months ago, and Julie wasn't overwhelmed by it now like she had been that first time, it was all about being prepared.

George waved at them and took Julie's hand to lead her into the hotel. The bellman held open the stately door and they found sanctuary inside.

'Sorry about that,' George apologised.

'No need to say sorry,' Julie smiled. She had been thumbing through every glossy magazine on board lately, hoping that she might get her fifteen minutes of fame through her famous beau.

'Sometimes I wish I wasn't famous, that I could just walk down the street and no one would recognise me, that's all.'

Julie looked at him, not knowing what to say. Until now he had seemed confident, like he was born famous, and could handle it, but it seemed he wanted to show her his vulnerable side, and she wasn't sure how she felt about that.

'Oh, but you would hate it really, just being a nobody, doing a boring job and earning pennies,' she said, trying to encourage him. He grinned back at her and sat up straight.

'You're right, what am I moaning about,' he said enthusiastically, leaning back in his seat and summoning the waiter. 'A bottle of your most expensive champagne please, it's the lady's birthday.'

Julie laughed, relieved to see this side of him back, she didn't want to get caught up in feelings again, they were dangerous...especially to her. 'That's better,' she said. She looked around the room and could see people at other tables looking at them, envying her, and she loved it. *Let them be jealous*, she thought with satisfaction, *because* today *I have everything I want.*

Chapter Sixteen

Ditching + 25:15hrs

Julie held her breath and watched as they emerged from the trees. As Ken moved aside she saw Laurence carrying something behind him and she stepped forward to meet them. Only when she got closer could she see that they were carrying Craig on a crude stretcher fashioned from branches.

'What happened?' Julie gasped, looking over the patient and seeing the blood stain on the cloth that was tied around his middle.

'I fell out of a tree,' Craig said weakly.

'We were lost, and trying to find our way back. Craig thought if he climbed up a tree he might be able to see the camp. I tried to stop him,' Laurence said, a hint of panic in his voice. 'He landed on some fallen branches, and one went into the side of his abdomen.'

''I'm okay, man,' Craig said, trying to sit up.

'Let us be the judge of that,' Julie said, gently pushing him back down and leading the group into the tent, where they placed the injured actor gently on the ground. 'Laurence, can you go over to my group and ask for Phil, he's a doctor,' Julie said. The rest of the crew had begun to arrive. It was just like on the plane, any hint of a medical situation and they were all straight on it. 'Jody, please find me some clean water, and a medical kit, we need to get this wound cleaned up before it gets infected.'

'I'm sure it's just a scratch,' said Craig. 'Although it did hurt.'

Julie started to unwrap the cloth that had been ripped from Ken's shirt she now recognised, looking up to see him standing there in just a vest, and for a second being distracted by the size of his biceps. She looked quickly back to what she was doing and tried to keep her face neutral as the wound was revealed, an ugly rip in his skin deep enough to show the layers of tissue beneath. Her first aid training was second to none, but while she had dealt with countless faints, burns, allergic reactions and cardiac arrest, wounds were rare onboard, and she had never seen one like this.

She looked closely and could see a small piece of wood protruding, splinters stuck into the flesh around it. There was no doubt it needed cleaning, and that the wood couldn't stay in there indefinitely, but right now she was extremely grateful to have a 'doctor on board,' so to speak, to make any decisions. On cue, Phil arrived, and Julie disregarded any previous dislike she had for him, because right now she needed his help.

As the doctor examined him, Julie stood up and walked over to the others. Laurence looked pale and she rubbed his arm gently.

'I couldn't carry him back, he was in too much pain, thank God you told us to take the flares,' he said.

'He's okay, it could have been worse,' Julie said.

'He was being a bit of a prick to be honest, talking about himself constantly the whole way, and showing off. I think he thought he was in a movie, but it didn't look like he'd ever climbed a tree in his life.' Laurence snorted, hiding his worry with contempt.

'He probably has a stunt double for anything dangerous,' Antonio said. 'Maybe I will teach him how to climb trees if we are stuck here much longer,' he added thoughtfully.

Julie remembered how Craig had been afraid of going out there, and could imagine him talking incessantly to cover up his nerves. Now she felt really guilty, she should have sent someone who was confident to go, not thrown him into it against his will.

It's your fault, you evil cow!

LOOK, look at him!

She looked over at him lying on the floor and felt terrible. The voices were right, if she hadn't made him go then he wouldn't have been there right now. She had been getting overconfident, believing she could direct this situation just because she had swallowed a manual, but perhaps she couldn't, perhaps she was letting everyone down.

You're weak, always have been, they need a leader, not you!

Julie let them carry on with their insults, they were right, indulging them until Milton's voice cut them off.

'I truly hope we aren't here much longer, the fish are cooking, but no one is going to be filled up at the end of it,' he said soberly. Julie had already decided that she could manage another day without food, the rumbling in her stomach was now a welcome distraction from the noise in her head.

'Ah, we found loads of mushrooms, they are in a blanket somewhere,' Laurence said, perking up and looking around him for his harvest. 'Edible ones too, before you worry.'

'That's great,' Milton said. 'Bring them on out and we'll get them cooking.'

'Fish and mushrooms for tea,' Julie said, surprised by how appetising the unlikely combination sounded right now.

'What a feast, bet the First-Class passengers will love it,' laughed Jody, passing them with a medical kit on her way to the patient. Her brightness made Julie smile, and the voices could never talk louder than a smile. She looked around and tried to find some perspective. Their plane had ditched and so far there was only one casualty; surely that was an achievement, surely she wasn't doing such a bad job?

She walked back over to watch as Phil professionally applied a clean dressing to Craig's torso. He was sitting up now and she could see how uncomfortable he was.

'I'm sorry for sending you out there, Craig,' Julie said. She could feel tears prick the back of her eyes.

'It's not your fault, you didn't push me out of the tree,' he said, looking back at her kindly, making her feel even worse.

'Now, take it easy, doctor's orders,' Phil said, patting him on the shoulder and standing up.

'Thanks, doc,' Craig said gratefully, pain etched on his face.

'Can I have a word?' Phil said, placing his hand on the small of Julie's back and guiding her away, out of earshot. Julie let him lead her, waiting for him to speak. 'I've cleaned it up the best I could, and given him some painkillers, but I can't risk removing the foreign body without knowing if it is penetrating anything important,' he said gravely.

'So, is it okay to just stay there?' Julie asked.

Phil shook his head. 'No, not for long, it will start to get infected, not to mention the pain the poor boy is in.' He looked at the ground for a moment before walking away.

'Well we had better hope that help arrives soon,' Julie said to no one in particular. She was starting to feel the pressure on their situation acutely now. No longer did they just hope for rescue, now they *needed* it.

Before he dies, and you're responsible for another death!

Julie put her hands over her ears and squeezed her eyes tightly shut, like she used to as a child. A hand touched her shoulder and made her jump and she opened her eyes to see Ken looking at her, his face full of concern. Without saying a word, he wrapped his strong arms around her and held her, letting her take some of his strength.

'Now, you're doing an awesome job, but it's okay not to be okay,' he said. Julie nodded, her forehead against his chest.

'Thank you,' she said, inhaling deeply before taking a step back and forcing a brave smile on her face. A single tear escaped and she brushed it away quickly.

'Any time,' he said, squeezing her shoulders with his strong hands and looking straight in her eyes for a moment before letting her go. 'Now I'm going back to the kitchen,' he smiled. 'Can you round up the diners?'

She nodded, grateful for someone giving *her* directions for once.

They ate fish and mushrooms with their fingers, from large leaves which had been cleaned with river water. Those that weren't selfish stood around and proclaimed that they weren't hungry, but Julie knew that like her, they were, they just chose to put others first. People talked to others that they hadn't met yet, having so far remained largely in their groups, and she was warmed by the scene as it unfolded. The human race was resilient if nothing else, she thought, and she had the utmost faith that they would all get out of this situation as better versions of the people who had boarded that plane. She looked across at Ken, who was watching her from his place at the side of the fire. He smiled at her and Julie smiled back, grateful that she had someone to lean on, even if it meant admitting her weaknesses once in a while.

'I'll just take this to Craig,' Laurence said as he walked past with a leaf of food.

'I'll take it for him,' Julie said, taking the meal from him, 'you go and get yourself something to eat.' She laid her spare hand on his shoulder and looked directly into his eyes. She could see his battle, his guilt and worry, she wasn't the only one battling the voices right now. 'Laurence, he's a grown man, you didn't make him climb that tree, and you couldn't have done more for him than you did.'

Laurence nodded sadly and released his grip on the food just as Cheryl passed them. 'Cheryl,' Julie called, getting her attention and summoning her over. 'When Laurence has got some food could you take him for a quick shot of medicine,' she winked. 'He needs something for the shock.'

'Oh yes, medicine,' Cheryl winked back. 'Come on, young man, we'll sort you out,' she said, taking a puzzled Laurence by the arm and leading him away. Julie watched Cheryl, who was getting more confident by the hour, and thought how she had found safety in their numbers, like she had herself once. On her way to the tent she passed Phil, who didn't even look up at her. His eyes were firmly fixed on his wife and his face was expressionless. She was grateful he was there to help her patient, but she couldn't shake off the contempt that she held for him.

Inside Craig lay alone, the tent deserted other than for him. His head was propped up on blankets and he looked okay, she thought, putting the food next to him and helping him to sit up.

'Here you go, some dinner,' she said as she handed him the offering. He took it from her, examining the peculiar dish and scratching his head. The action made Julie laugh.

'I know, it's not your average First Class meal, but it was the best we could do,' she said.

'The strangest meal I've ever had,' he said, poking it with his finger. 'Do I use my fingers?' Julie nodded, watching him gingerly pick up a mushroom and pop it in his mouth. He chewed, a thoughtful expression on his face which eventually turned into one of approval. 'Not bad.'

Julie's mouth watered as she watched him. She was used to being a little bit hungry, always watching her weight, but now she was *really* hungry.

'Do you want some?' He must have read her thoughts, holding out what was left of his food.

'Oh, no thank you,' she waved off the offer. 'I've had some,' she lied. 'So, tell me about yourself, Craig. Who are you looking forward to getting back to?' She remembered back to the raft when he was talking to someone on his phone.

'My dog,' he said with a smile, surprising Julie.

'No girlfriend?' she asked. He shook his head.

'No,' he laughed and took another bite of his food. 'For one I'm gay, and two, it's too hard having a relationship when you're famous. It never works.'

'Yes, I've heard that,' she said knowingly, and she did know first-hand. 'Too many good offers, hey?'

He looked surprised by her comment, shaking his head. 'No, not at all. It's just too intense for most people, that level of scrutiny. I haven't found anyone who can handle it yet. So I live with my parents and my dog in the middle of nowhere. I am forever lonely.' He shrugged with a half-smile as he concentrated on picking up the fish that was flaking apart between his fingers.

Julie hadn't expected his response, or to feel sorry for the boy she had apparently misjudged. If she took one thing away from this situation when she got back to normal life, it would be *never* to prejudge anyone again, especially when you were making those judgements based on things that had happened to you.

'How are you?' Laurence was standing there now, looking much better, and Julie wondered if Cheryl had administered him some 'medicine.'

'Good, thank you,' Craig smiled.

'I'll leave you to keep Craig company, Laurence,' Julie said, getting up.

Emerging from the tent she noticed how the daylight was fading and she began to feel panicked again. They couldn't stay here another night! No, the pilots had to get back, they needed to get Craig to hospital, Bet needed to get some proper food, Reuben needed nappies…. She felt her thoughts spiralling downwards and looked around for Ken to calm her. Unable to see him anywhere she walked over to Milton, who was leaning over poking the fire with a stick and adding more wood to it. She stood back a little to avoid the burning embers that were scattering as he did it.

'Milton, have you seen Ken?' she asked, hoping he couldn't hear the anxiety in her voice.

'He's gone down to the lake,' he said over his shoulder. 'Something about tying some lifejackets to the trees where the boats landed.'

'Ah, okay,' Julie said, that made sense, but she hoped he was back before it got dark as she would need him if they had to stay another night. 'Did he go on his own?'

'No, he took Antonio with him.'

'Just Antonio?'

'I think so.' Milton had stood up now and was looking at her properly.

Julie wondered why Antonio hadn't insisted they go as a three, he knew the same rules as her, what was he thinking?

'They'll be fine,' Milton said kindly. 'Stop worrying.'

'Is it that obvious?' she asked.

'Yes, and understandable, but we've got this.' He had his hand on her shoulder and was looking right into her eyes just as Ken had, talking her down in exactly the same way. 'Okay?'

Julie nodded. 'Thank you, Milton,' she said gratefully, comforted both by his words and by the fact that a second person had shown the ability to calm her down in such a short space of time. Where had these people been all her life?

Julie turned and watched as people began to get up and move back into the tent, leaving their dinner leaves full of fish bones scattered around the floor. Instinctively the crew had begun picking them up, clearing in the dinner service in this new class of cabin. Even now the majority of passengers were still behaving like passengers, and the uniformed crew were still behaving like crew. Julie observed the scene with some amusement, glad that there were a few exceptions in the group, that some of them had become as much a part of their survival as the crew were… and for them she would be eternally grateful.

Chapter Seventeen

12 years earlier

'**A**re you coming out for drinks tonight, Julie?' asked Kyle.

'Of course she is,' called Rosie over her shoulder as she left the galley with a tray full of food.

'Of course,' Julie echoed, answering for herself. Things had changed since she had taken back control of her life. She was happier, and an effect of that was that her crew loved her, wanting her to join them at their room parties or at the bar again; she was great company apparently. These days Julie walked around with a smile on her face, and the smile had silenced the voices.

'I can't wait for the rum punch,' said Kyle, as he arranged a mediocre salmon dinner to look like a work of art on the plate.

'Ooh yes, I do love a rum punch on arrival,' Julie agreed, picturing the hotel lobby with the path leading from the front right down to the beach, and the waiter holding a tray of cocktails for them. Barbados, her favourite destination.

'Better top up that tan for your next magazine shoot,' Rosie said walking back into the galley, the food replaced with a tower of dirty plates on her tray. Julie laughed as Rosie explained to Kyle.

'She's dating George Downing, and was in *YES* magazine with him last month.'

Kyle's eyes were wide as he turned away from his food preparation to look at her. 'Seriously?'

'It's nothing serious, we just go on dates occasionally,' Julie said. Rosie was right though, she had finally found a picture of herself in a glossy magazine, being ushered into a restaurant by George. It certainly wasn't a 'shoot' though, not like they were a celebrity couple, more that he had been 'papped' with a mystery woman, and she was the envy of his army of fans.

'You go, girl!' Kyle said, obviously impressed.

Jack came back into the galley from the opposite aisle, exhaling loudly. 'Seriously, just because this is a non-stop flight, my lot think it's a non-stop service,' he muttered under his breath.

'Well it will make the flight go quickly if we are busy,' Julie replied, relieving him of his heavily laden tray and giving him an empty one in return.

'Thanks, sorry, man trouble,' he apologised.

'That's fine, men are always trouble in a relationship, how you boys manage when there are two of you in one is beyond me,' Julie quipped, as she sorted the dirty plates and cutlery into plastic drawers.

As the service dwindled to an end, Julie took a walk down through the cabin to see how things were going at the back.

'Here, let me help you,' she said to the man who was trying to get in the toilet. She slowly pushed at the exact point where it said 'PUSH', opening the door for him with ease whilst wondering why so many passengers seemed unable to work it out.

'Thanks,' he said, stepping inside without looking at her.

'You're welcome,' she said politely, sensing his embarrassment.

None of the crew were in the aisles and she was pleased to see that the dinner trays were cleared in, signalling that their service was over too and that they might be able to squeeze some crew rest in, because she was feeling particularly tired today for some reason.

When she walked into the back galley the crew were all standing with their backs to her and she got closer to see what they were doing. Empty miniature bottles were piled up on one end of the galley side as two of them poured the contents of others into empty water bottles... bus-juice was being prepared! Julie was looking forward to a cocktail on the bus to the hotel as much as anyone, but she was also aware that any passenger could have walked in and seen this, and they would all be in trouble if they were reported.

'Girls,' she said, amused by how they all froze for a moment before turning around in the most awkward manner, trying to hide their project. 'Perhaps draw the curtain and make sure no one sees you.' They all nodded, faces crimson, and she could see the fear in their eyes that they had just been caught out and might be in trouble. Julie smiled as she turned and pulled the curtain across behind her as she left, popping her head back through one last time.

'Oh, if you could arrange a nice bottle of gin and tonic, chilled, that would be great... and don't forget the plastic glasses,' she added with a wink and a grin.

****

Music played through a speaker that Kyle had had the foresight to pack, as the girls poured out cocktails to everyone on the shabby bus that was taking them through the bumpy streets to their hotel.

'Thank you very much,' Julie said, taking the plastic glass of gin and tonic and sipping it. 'Wow, that's strong,' she winced as she swallowed it, not enjoying the taste as much as she had anticipated. What was wrong with her taste buds? She liked *any* gin in *any* measure usually. Persevering with the rest of the glass she watched out of the window as they drove along the coast, the turquoise blue sea stretched out to the horizon. Then through the painted houses that lined the dusty streets, and past the opening to St Laurence Gap, the famous street that would be bustling with holidaymakers later, once the sun had set and the bars turned up their reggae music.

Up the hill they continued until they reached their hotel and the bus driver pulled in to let them off. Finding her suitcase at the back of the bus Julie moved into the shaded open-air lobby. She looked down the path to the glistening water and gazed at it for a moment. She had packed her new bikini and she had a firm date with a sunbed first thing tomorrow morning.

'Rum punch, miss,' the man said, holding the tray of delicious cocktails out to her.

'I should think so,' Julie smiled, taking the glass that looked the fullest. 'Thank you, James,' she said, noting the name on his badge. She had learned that it was always a good idea to make friends with the staff, happy hour could generally be extended if you knew the right people.

'Okay, down in the bar in forty-five minutes,' the captain called from the reception desk, key already in his hand. That was more than enough time for Julie, she had a slick routine that didn't cut any glamour corners and ensured she always arrived looking her best in minimal time. She was older than the average crew member now, but she didn't have to look it!

****

Julie woke up to darkness, the sound of the waves outside of her open balcony doors reminding her of where she was. She looked down to see that she was still in her uniform and the clock told her that it was already seven-thirty, two hours since they had arrived. She got up swiftly, trying not to rush, knowing that they would all still be there for hours. It was fine, she thought, jumping in the shower to wash the scent of aircraft off her quickly. As she applied her makeup she wondered what had happened, it wasn't like her to fall asleep like that, she had only meant to close her eyes for a minute. Perhaps this was what it was like when you got to middle-age, she mulled, unimpressed but amused nevertheless by the explanation. Well, she didn't look middle-aged, she argued, looking at the person in the mirror. She was starting to embrace the sixties starlet look: blonde hair always backcombed and fixed high, fringe swept to the sides to frame her face, red lipstick and kohl eyes, it suited her. Her petite figure was wrapped in a strappy floral dress, wedged heels elongating her legs which she had polished and tanned the night before.

She could hear the steel band playing from the bar now and animated voices from down below as she pulled her glass doors shut and locked them. The party might have started without her, but she was ready to make her entrance and make up for what she had missed.

'Julieeee,' called Kyle as she walked around the pool to the bar. She recognised his obvious state of inebriation, in fact the whole group of crew that were sitting around the table had exaggerated smiles on their faces…

'I'll be over in a minute,' she called back, stepping up to the bar.

'What can I get for you, miss?' It was James from earlier.

'Two of your best rum punches please, James,' she said, needing to catch up with the others.

Scooping up two glasses of ice, James poured the orangey-red punch straight from the five-gallon jerrycan in which it had been premixed. He added the obligatory maraschino cherry and grated a little nutmeg on top, before setting them down in front of her with a big smile on his face. As he looked down at the till, Julie picked up the one nearest to her and quickly gulped it down through the straw, pushing the empty glass back on the bar, much to the amusement of James as he looked back up.

'I have some catching up to do,' she said with a wink, signing the bill and picking up the other glass.

The crew, who all looked so different now with their hair down and summer clothes on, shuffled along and made room for Julie to join them on one of the sofas.

'Sorry I'm late,' she apologised. 'Did I miss much?'

'No, we were just talking about you actually,' one of the girls said, raising her eyebrows. Julie leaned her head to the side, intrigued as to why she had been the topic of conversation.

'So, Julie, when do we get to meet George?' Kyle asked loudly across the table, directing everyone's attention to her.

Ah, thought Julie, *that is why.*

'Julie dates George Downing,' he announced to those who hadn't been privy to the information before. Everyone was now listening in, and Julie took a big gulp of her drink before answering.

'Erm, never?!' she said and laughed. 'We aren't serious, it's just an odd date.'

'So how long have you been dating him?' Rosie asked sweetly.

'About a year,' Julie said thoughtfully; yes about a year was right.

'A year and it's not serious?' Kyle snorted. 'It sounds serious enough to me.'

Julie smiled. 'No, it suits me, being with someone famous could be a drag.' She had seen that first hand, how they could never just pop in somewhere, they only went to places where rich and famous people went, where they were shielded from the public and the paparazzi, normal life just not worth the trouble. She told herself that she liked normal life, that she would miss it.

'So, if he proposed you'd say no?' Kyle asked, making Julie splutter with the directness of his question.

'Yes, I'd say no, and he'd never ask. Honestly, guys, it is just a bit of fun. Please keep it to yourselves,' she pleaded. The relationship, not that it qualified as one, suited her just fine without the pressures of this kind of speculation. She'd had her little bit of fame, but that had been enough for her and she had been pleasantly surprised that she didn't yearn for more.

'Well you know what these actors are like, he's probably got half a dozen on the go anyway,' a gruff voice interrupted from the far end of the table. Julie looked at the captain, who was sitting with an amused and unkind expression on his face. She looked at his swollen red nose, sitting in the middle of his chubby face with its pitted skin. His second chin met his chest, which led to his oversized stomach, the buttons of his shirt finding it a challenge to hold it together. She held his stare until he looked away, knowing that an intelligent man wouldn't say something so obviously cutting if he didn't mean to cause offence, and she felt a strong urge to throw what was left of her punch over his thinning grey hair. He didn't seem to care that all conversation had stopped and everyone had heard his remark, looking back at them nonchalantly and shrugging his shoulders. 'Well it was a stupid question, don't you think? He's hardly likely to propose to her, is he?'

Julie shook her head slowly and turned her back on him so that only her crew could see her rolling her eyes. They were all clearly shocked and embarrassed for her, but she was neither, she had seen this behaviour before.

'Just ignore him, he's clearly a friend of my ex-husband's,' she said. Paul had done a good job of blackening her name amongst the pilots after the divorce, getting in there first before she could blacken his with the true facts. Despite the obvious lies which they were blinkered enough to believe, she couldn't even be bothered to try to educate such pompous bigots.

'There was no need for that though,' Kyle said, offended on her behalf.

'Honestly, ignore him,' she said, 'I am.' She held up her almost empty glass to get James's attention, and he nodded back from behind the bar in understanding of her request for another drink. 'He's just a sad old man.'

'Here,' Kyle said, leaning down beneath his seat and taking out a water bottle from a duty-free bag that lay there. 'Have this while you are waiting,' he said, and filled her glass with the remains of the bus-juice.

'Thank you,' she said gratefully.

Julie knew why he had been so unkind, and perhaps his words were true, but honestly she was happy with her arrangement with George, she told herself. So why had it made a tiny cut in her feelings?

Ditched

****

The phone ringing startled Julie.

'Hello,' she said, wondering whose groggy voice it was speaking – it didn't sound like her own.

'Your wakeup call, madam,' said a lady with a Caribbean accent.

Julie looked at the receiver and then at her clock. 'Thank you,' she said, hanging up in disbelief. Never in all of her years of flying had she slept through until the afternoon, and missed her date with a sunbed! She stumbled around, uncoordinated for a while and having to force herself to focus and get herself together; she had forty-five minutes to get down to reception, and right now the sixties starlet had been replaced by an eighties rock chick in the mirror. She had enjoyed the evening but it had ended when the bar had shut at midnight, so that wasn't the reason for her marathon sleep, and surely middle-aged women didn't need to sleep for fourteen hours a night, how would they ever get anything done?!

She got in the shower, turning it to a lower temperature than she would normally have, feeling the tepid water on her face waking her up. She lathered up her sponge and washed her body down, refreshing her skin with vigorous scrubbing. An unexpected tenderness when she washed her breasts stopped her for a moment, it was a sensitivity she hadn't felt before. She touched them, feeling a hardness that even her menstrual cycle didn't usually evoke. That thought caused her stomach to flip as she thought hard to pinpoint today's date – July 10th – and she thought back to her last period. When was that? Back she went through her flights and other memorable dates, trying to remember if she had had it on any of them, but she just couldn't recall. She ran her palm over her stomach, still slightly bloated from yesterday's flight – that wasn't unusual was it?

Julie stood frozen, as the water pummelled her. Her womb was useless, wasn't it? She couldn't get pregnant, could she? She shook her head and stepped out of the shower, looking at her body in the mirror, wondering if it only looked different now because of her thoughts. She shook her head and picked the towel up from the floor and started drying herself manically. There was absolutely nothing she could do about anything right now, she thought firmly, calling on all of her strength and stoicism to get herself ready and through tonight's flight, she would have to worry about it tomorrow.

You've gone and got yourself pregnant, haven't you?

You stupid cow!

Chapter Eighteen

Ditching + 27:30hrs

Julie knew she was pacing, that she was beginning to panic, that things were starting to fall apart. She couldn't think clearly, the voices were even jumbled up to the extent that she couldn't understand them anymore, which wasn't necessarily a bad thing. It was nearly dark now and no one had come back, not Ken and Antonio, or the captain and Derren. Surely, they should have found help by now?

'Right, you and I are going on a break.'

It was Cheryl, holding her by the elbow and leading her into the trees.

'Now, forgive me if I'm speaking out of turn, but it certainly looks like you could do with some of this.' She pulled the gin bottle out from under the bush and handed it to Julie. Julie held it up and noticed that there was still half a bottle left, not bad considering. She unscrewed the top and took a sip, and then more, before handing it back.

'They will be back soon, and we will get rescued soon, but you need to get some sleep, lady, and switch off for a few hours.'

Julie nodded, she knew she was right, that she had barely slept the night before and that she was exhausted from being on alert for so long now.

'I just want to wait until Ken and Antonio come back,' she said, knowing that she couldn't possibly sleep before then.

'They will be back before you know it, but why don't you go and close your eyes for a minute and I'll wake you up as soon as they arrive,' Cheryl said persuasively. Julie could feel the gin relaxing her now, and things started to feel less 'sped-up.' She nodded in agreement, following her new friend back towards the tent. As they emerged from the bushes Julie stumbled and landed on her knees by a fallen tree. She felt something fall and land beside her. Picking it up she noticed that it was the radio beacon; Iain must have put it there for some unbeknown reason, she thought, studying it. She carried it with her into the light of the fire which was burning brightly now night had fallen.

Looking at the top of it she scrunched her eyes up to read the words. The toggle switch was in the TEST position, having long ago performed its self-test, and had obviously been sitting idle ever since.

'Stupid man,' Julie groaned under her breath, flipping the switch to ON and placing it back up on the highest branch she could reach. Tomorrow she would send Antonio to put it up higher still, if he ever came back.

'We are back.' His voice cut through the air just on cue, Julie and Cheryl turning to see the two men emerging from behind a stream of torchlight. Julie felt the relief flood over her, standing still with a smile fixed on her face as she watched the others greet them. Ken looked over and saw her watching, walking over to where she was.

'I was getting worried,' she said quietly.

'Sorry, we took a bit longer as your crew member wanted to do it properly, he was like a monkey up those trees,' he grinned.

'I found the radio beacon,' she said, filling him in on what he had missed, 'the captain hadn't switched it on, but it is set now.'

'Well they should find us in the morning then,' Ken said confidently. Julie realised Ken had just confirmed her fear that they were spending another night here, and she felt a wave of acceptance. She was sure that Craig would survive a night, and that Reuben wouldn't starve, as long as it was just one more. She could hear a baby crying, and her heart ached for him and how helpless his parents must be feeling. As she walked back over she saw him in his father's arms as the three of them came outside, trying to console him with the night air.

'We will be out of here in the morning, I am sure of it,' Julie said to Chloe, knowing that the measures they had taken this evening had certainly given them the best chance now. She tried not to let herself imagine what might have happened to the pilots, as her thoughts were threatening to become dark as the tiredness set in. Reuben had stopped crying now, and Julie breathed in his aura. 'Can I watch him for you?' she offered.

'That would be lovely,' Luke said, handing the now sleeping, blanket-wrapped bundle to her.

Julie carried the baby into the tent and found a quiet corner. Using a rolled-up blanket to rest her head on she lay down on her side on the floor with him tucked in her arm, her body wrapped around him. She closed her eyes, prepared for the rush of thoughts and worries that would keep her awake, but they didn't come. In his sweet innocence Reuben acted as an invisible force field against the darkness and Julie slipped peacefully into the deepest sleep.

****

An unfamiliar sound woke Julie, the sound of a baby making happy noises. She opened her eyes and saw Reuben staring up into the darkness that filled the tent and cooing. Chloe came into focus and sat cross-legged next to her, smiling down at them both. Julie sat up, her hips aching from lying on the hard floor.

Ditched

'I'm sorry, I stole your baby,' she apologised, 'you should have taken him. How long were we asleep?'

'A few hours. You were both so peaceful I didn't have the heart to disturb you,' Chloe said quietly, the rest of the tent silent apart from the obligatory one person snoring loudly as always.

'Here, thank you so much for letting me borrow him, that was the best sleep I think I have ever had,' said Julie, reluctantly handing him back to his mother.

'Yep, he has that effect.' Chloe lifted him up in the air, evoking a huge gummy smile. 'Shall we go and see Daddy? You need to go back to sleep after a little feed, young man,' she said, standing up. 'Thank you for looking after him, you are so good with babies you know, it's such a shame you never had your own.'

Julie smiled back but she didn't say anything, she had no words at that moment. She watched as they walked away, aching not to have the little bundle of comfort taken away. She got up, feeling older than her age, and reached for the small torch that always hung from her belt loop on flights. She shone it on her watch, making out that by the time zone she presumed they were in it was about two a.m. She couldn't sleep any more though, and felt quite refreshed considering it had only been a few short hours. It was amazing how you could adapt to the lack of comforts when you needed to, she mused. Her stomach rumbled, and she put her hand over it to silence it.

Julie followed the narrow path that her torch illuminated towards the tent's entrance. It was chilly by the door, but she could hear the crackle of the fire outside that would soon warm her up. Something told her to quickly check on her group, and she backtracked slightly over to the area which they had claimed.

Everyone was lying around seemingly asleep; only Chloe was awake, lying with her family, feeding Reuben. She smiled to see that Ken and Milton had finally given in and taken some rest themselves, Milton emitting a soft snore as he lay on his back near the outskirts of the shelter. The torch moved past Anna and Ruby, to Phil, sleeping on his own. Cheryl was on the other side of the group, keeping her safe distance. Eric and Bet lay on their backs side by side holding hands; Julie wished she could have given them something more comfortable to lie on, knowing that their aged bones must be suffering with the hardness of the floor even worse than hers had.

Her torch landed on Craig, and she knelt down next to him. He was sleeping but his breath sounded laboured, as if he was in pain still. She placed one hand lightly on his forehead and felt the clamminess of his skin, cold to the touch. Years of first aid had given her an instinct about when people were really sick as opposed to just overtired and emotional, and Craig was battling right now.

He opened his eyes as she took her hand away and gave her a small smile.

'We'll be out of here today,' she said, and she had to believe it herself, because what would happen if they weren't didn't bear thinking about.

Outside, Laurence kept watch with Max and Jake, and Julie sat quietly with them. The animated conversations from the night before had been replaced by silence as they each contemplated the situation they were in. Sitting on the floor with her knees hugged to her chest Julie closed her eyes on and off until finally the birds began to chirp as dawn arrived. She smiled at the songs they were singing, at first to silence the voices that had been whispering on and off throughout the night, and then because she heard hope in their callings. She stood up and breathed in deeply, the fresh air filling her lungs and delivering oxygen to her body. Yes, she thought as she stretched out her arms, today was going to be a good day. Today was going to be the day they got out of here, she had no doubt of it in her mind.

Chapter Nineteen

12 years earlier

The rollercoaster was the worst she had ever ridden, albeit in her mind. She had taken the test three times, just to make sure, and each time it had told her that she was pregnant. For years she had thought it was her that couldn't have a baby, but it must have been Paul all along.

So, she was pregnant, and now what? Did she want a baby? Of course she did! But was she too old? She was over forty now, but plenty of women were leaving it later these days, weren't they? Once the shock had worn off she hadn't been able to stop smiling.

'I can confirm you are approximately eleven weeks pregnant,' the lovely doctor had said. 'I have to ask, but I think I know the answer, are you planning to go through with the pregnancy?'

She had nodded vigorously, aware of the stupid smile that was still stuck to her face, leaving the surgery and going straight to Mothercare to start looking at baby things.

Now as she stood in front of the mirror in her apartment she ran her hand over her small bump, invisible to anyone but her, and she suddenly felt nervous. The buzzer rang and she let George in, opening her front door to a huge bunch of flowers behind which came the unwitting father-to-be. She accepted his kiss and his hug; it had been over six weeks since their last date, and she was glad that he seemed pleased to see her.

'Champagne please,' George ordered as soon as they sat at the table in the Ivy. The waiters all seemed to know him, he had obviously been here many times before, and a moment of unsettlement surprised Julie when she thought he might have been bringing other girls here these past six weeks.

'Can I just get a sparkling water, please,' she called after the waiter as he walked away. Craig looked at her with a confused expression. 'I'm detoxing,' she added by way of explanation.

'It's cool, more for me,' he smiled, and she was glad that he didn't care that she wasn't drinking champagne with him, as long as he could.

Over dinner they made small talk, with her mostly listening to him talk about his latest film and dropping in names of celebrities that he was going to be working with.

She had never noticed before how much he loved to talk about himself, how little they spoke about her. Probably it had suited her before, but right now she sat impatiently listening and waiting for the right moment to turn the conversation onto the current situation.

'Would you like dessert, madam?' the waiter asked, clearing away their plates.

'No, thank you,' Julie said, as much as she would have loved a slice of whatever that delicious-looking work of art was that he had just delivered to the table next door.

'Watching your figure?' George winked at her, ordering himself something. He was getting quite merry now, and she was starting to find his self-absorption quite irritating if she was truthful. She wondered if he was getting worse as he got more successful, or if she had just not noticed it before when she was drinking along with him.

'I'm sorry, I am just talking about me, what's been happening with you?'

His apology and subsequent question came unexpectedly and startled Julie, and suddenly everything she had planned to say had escaped her mind. He was half way to being drunk, she could see though, and she realised that she would have to say something sooner rather than later, speaking quickly before he had a chance to go back to his favourite subject, him. 'Would you like children one day, George?'

He sat back and looked thoughtful, accepting her question as if she were interviewing him. 'I guess so, yeah, that would be nice. Some little ones running up to see me when I get home from filming.'

He was smiling, a thoughtful look on his face and she took this as a good sign, pursuing the subject some more.

'What would you like, girls or boys?' she asked casually, taking a sip of her water.

'Erm, two of each,' he said after a moment.

'Wow, four children, you must really like the idea.' She felt a glimmer of hope that this might end well, although she had prepared herself for either outcome.

'Yeah, maybe one day, but not yet,' he grinned at her, quashing her hopes in those last two little words.

'Well then, you might not like what I am going to tell you,' she began, remembering and starting the speech that she had been preparing all day. 'I'm pregnant, George, but it's fine if you don't want to be involved, I plan on keeping the baby but I am okay with doing it on my own so you don't have to worry.' Her words tumbled out without control, clumsily, but she could see that he had understood her.

George was staring at her with his mouth open; she wanted to lean over and push his lower jaw up, but instead she took his glass and drank a mouthful of his champagne. One mouthful would not hurt her unborn child more than sobriety was hurting her right now, she reasoned.

'Wow,' George said eventually. 'I hadn't expected that.' He seemed sober all of a sudden, and his face was pale.

'Look, I think this is a lot for you to take in,' Julie said after a minute or so of sitting in silence, George looking everywhere but at her. She stood up and pushed her chair in, picking her bag up from the table. 'I will go on home and leave you to think about it, you have my number.' She could see now that it wasn't something they could talk through together, that they just weren't that sort of couple; indeed they weren't a couple at all.

Standing outside on the pavement waiting for a taxi, she imagined him coming running out, telling her not to go, that they could make it work… but that was all it was, her imagination. How could they commit to raising a child together when he was still a child himself? He didn't even know her real age for heaven's sake, such was the shallowness of their relationship, and she understood that clearer than ever now. She watched the couples that walked along the street, and into the restaurant, they just weren't like them, and up until now that had been fine with her, but it just wasn't enough now.

Well that's that then, a single mother…

You weren't good enough for him to settle down with….

The voices mocked her as she sat in the taxi, and she dug deep to remember how she had felt positive about it up until now, how she had known she could do it on her own, how she was going to be a great mum…

Ditched

As she walked into her apartment her phone buzzed, and she sat down to read George's message:

Dear Julie,

I'm really sorry but I'm not ready for this, I had presumed you had taken precautions. I ask you to think about the implications of doing this alone as I would not want the press to find out, or there be a child in the world that thinks its dad doesn't care if I am removed from the situation. Perhaps it would be best to think about a termination, I am happy to pay to have you seen privately. I will send a cheque to cover the costs should you need it. Take care and I wish you all the best for your future, George.

He hadn't even slept on it, hadn't even taken the time to weigh it up, just gone straight into getting rid of the baby. Julie's finger hovered over the delete button, knowing that this was the last she would hear from George, that he had done exactly what she had deep-down known he would do. She took a deep breath and composed herself. It was fine, she would be enough for their baby, although his reference to a child thinking its dad didn't care needed more thought. She rubbed her stomach and took in what had just happened.

Haha, you just got DITCHED!!

They were cackling like the evillest of witches.

'Oh, FUCK OFF!' Julie shouted aloud to them. She might have been ditched, but she was going to have a baby, it had been worth it. She smiled, and they fell silent.

Chapter Twenty

Ditching + 41:00hrs

The humming noise was getting louder, bringing the majority of the survivors out into the open. Everyone looked to the sky and it seemed to Julie that, like herself, no one was breathing. As the stub nose of the light aircraft appeared above the trees not far in the distance, Julie's arms flew into the air of their own accord, waving frantically. Suddenly everyone was shouting, waving, whistling, all united in their attempt to get the pilot's attention.

They watched as the plane banked and turned away just before it got over their heads and the shouts raised to deafening levels as they tried to call it back; but as their calls faded so did the noise from the engine as it flew away.

The adrenaline coursed through Julie's body, and she could feel her heart beating hard inside her chest. She clenched her fists by her side as she willed the pilot to come back, to come just a fraction more in their direction, to SEE them. Still the engine got quieter and they all fell silent again. Time stood still, a few short minutes feeling like eternal hours, and the air got heavy as the remaining bubbles of hope burst and fell to earth. Julie felt an arm on her shoulder, and as she became aware of herself again she realised that she was crying, that big fat tears were streaming down her face. She wiped them away, willing them to stop coming, but they wouldn't.

Julie glanced left and right at the people closest to her, seeing her own despair mirrored in their faces, and sucked in a deep breath, filling her lungs with oxygen. She couldn't fall apart now, she was responsible for these people, and if *she* started giving up hope what would they do? She pulled herself away from the well-meant arm, turning to see Milton looking down at her.

'I'm fine,' she said, wiping the last tear away. 'Thank you.'

'They'll be back soon,' he said with assurance.

'Yes,' Julie said, 'they will be.' She had to believe it.

'Julie, Craig's not doing so well,' Cheryl approached them. 'Phil's with him now, but he really needs to get some antibiotics soon.'

Julie nodded; it wasn't anything she didn't know, but she was helpless, no use to him whatsoever. She looked around at the people who stood in small groups and wondered how many of them were missing meds that they needed, were hiding their personal sufferings because they knew there was nothing anyone could do?

She could hear Reuben crying again, and the sound echoed her own internal wails. She shuddered, trying to shake it off, to go back to that moment this morning when she had been so sure it was going to be a good day. After all, they had the beacon on now… but what if it wasn't working? They had left signs by the water though, surely somebody would see them? And the pilots… they must have found someone by now?

'Julie.' The voice was muffled and Julie realised her hands were over her ears, trying to quieten her mind. Embarrassed, she took them away and opened her eyes. Ken was standing next to Milton and they were both looking at her with kindness on their faces, making her want to cry even more.

'They *will* be back,' Ken said assuredly, and something about the way he said it breathed new hope into Julie, she believed him. She looked to Milton, who was nodding in agreement, and she could see that they were both in no doubt about it. She started to nod along with them, wiping her face dry again and trying her hardest to smile back.

'Sorry, gentlemen, I was just having a wobble,' she apologised. Ken opened his mouth to say something, shutting it again abruptly and looking up. The humming was coming back, getting louder again, and everyone fell back into silence as it got closer. The plane's nose appeared, then the two propeller engines, the noise of which was soon drowned out by the shouts and screams of the crowd, who were even more determined this time to be heard. Julie was silent though, unmoving, too afraid to even think in case she couldn't cope with the disappointment if they didn't see them.

In slow motion it kept coming towards them, just above the canopy of the trees, flying right over their heads before banking to the right and flying away.

'Did they see us?' she asked quietly to no one in particular.

'I think so,' said Ken as they all still looked upwards and listened to the engines getting further away, and then begin to get louder again as the plane completed its circle and came back towards them.

This time when it appeared above the trees it rocked its wings twice, the sign that Julie and her crew all knew meant they had been seen, and this time Julie let the tears flow as her lips trembled into a huge smile. The camp erupted into cheers and Julie felt weightless, a crushing band around her chest. Ken had wrapped his arms around her and lifted her into the air. He spun her around and around before finally putting her back down, dizzy and elated. Julie didn't know what to do with herself, but it didn't matter because this time it was Milton who picked her up and spun her around. The three of them laughed out loud, relief turning into euphoria all around them as people hugged and danced. A tap on her shoulder from Eric, a hug from Cheryl, the mutual tears that spoke a thousand words from Chloe, Julie was so overwhelmed with the happiness and love being sent her way she was afraid that she might explode.

'Right, we had best get prepared to be rescued,' she said finally, decisively, once the plane had gone; now that they knew where they were it surely couldn't be long until the rescuers arrived. So, she thought as she strode quickly towards the tent, what exactly did that entail? Did they need to pack up, or could they leave that to someone else? She would need to make a list of the most vulnerable, yes, that was a good start, in case they had to be taken out a few at a time.... Her mind raced as she wondered how they would be rescued, by boat? Winched up into a helicopter? Or was there a road just a short distance away all along?

Julie stood at the tent's doorway and didn't know what to do first. She imagined the rescuers arriving, and she pictured how she would greet them, how she would be professional and dignified, a credit to the airline's safety training department. She would be in the newspapers no doubt, and perhaps they would want to interview her on television one day... Julie walked quickly, now knowing her immediate priority, grabbing her makeup bag and finding a quiet corner. They were going to be rescued, and she was not going to be met by their heroes, or worst still, photographed, looking like she did right now!

Chapter Twenty-One

12 years earlier

T he Botox was wearing off and struggling to fight the lines around her eyes, that were being formed by the smile which had been fixed to Julie's face for weeks now. She didn't care though, glancing at her reflection as she passed the mirror. She was glowing, happiness radiated from her, everyone said so, and she wouldn't be injecting or putting anything unhealthy into her body for the foreseeable future.

She sat down behind the desk, rubbing her stomach that was now beginning to round as her baby grew inside it.

'Julie, no way!!' Julie looked up to see a face she recognised but couldn't for the life of her remember the girl's name. 'Congratulations! When are you due?'

'Twentieth of September,' Julie said, beaming, the date so ingrained in her mind now, even though it was still over four months away.

'I can't believe it, I'm so happy for you.' The girl was clearly thrilled, and Julie really wished she could at least remember where they had flown, trying to read her name badge without being obvious. 'Do you know what you're having?'

'Not yet, I'll find out at my scan next week,' she said.

Next week she would know if she was having a son or a daughter. She was absolutely bursting to find out, not that it mattered in the slightest to her which it was, but she was desperate to add the finishing touches to the nursery and add some cute outfits to the already full baby closet.

'How exciting,' the girl said. 'I'd better go, my briefing is just starting. Congratulations again.'

'Thanks,' Julie said with a smile, turning back to the pile of flight reports that she had to get through before her shift finished. Life behind the 'bump desk' was fun for a change, different to flying, the job given to the girls that were grounded when they were pregnant, those affectionately known as 'The Bumps.' Only the smallest part of her felt envious as she watched the crews coming and going, off to go shopping in New York or drink cocktails in Cuba. She would be back in the skies one day, but not in a hurry. No, she had it all planned, a year of maternity leave and then she would get an au pair or a nanny that could look after her child a couple of times a month while she went back to work. She could just about afford it, and if she couldn't then George would have to help, whether he liked it or not. So far she hadn't contacted him, but she wouldn't be letting their child go without because of misplaced pride. Nothing mattered apart from this little life, and if he didn't want to be a father that was fine, but financial help was a whole other matter.

Julie picked up the pile of passenger manifests and walked over to the shredder. The black trouser suit they had given her was still huge and rendered her shapeless, yet she had never felt more beautiful.

'Can I give you these to shred after?'

'Of course,' Julie said, turning around and holding out her empty hand. The look on Paul's face when he recognised her was priceless, and she took a mental photo of it for her memories. She could practically see the demons dance behind his eyes, and she wondered if he had voices too, such was his tortured look. Hers had been long silent since she had found her happiness, but Paul looked ashen, and she wondered what it was about seeing her that made him so grave. Was it the memory of the times he had hurt her, or the way she had called him out on it? Or was it the fact that she was standing here right now in front of him as proof of his failure at being a man, proof that it was he who couldn't father children all along?

'Oh hi, Paul, nice to see you. How are you?' she said brightly, surprised how her heart rate barely raised, and how confident she felt, after actively avoiding him these past few years.

'Good thanks, er, congratulations,' he said awkwardly, pushing the papers into her hand and taking a step back. 'Got to go.'

Julie watched as he walked quickly along the corridor to where the pilots were briefed, laughing to herself. She hadn't thought about Paul for such a long time, and any feelings she had once had for him were long gone. She had been as surprised to see him then as he had been to see her, but she had definitely handled it best. In fact, Julie could handle anything right now; this little being had given her immeasurable strength, and clarity that she had never had in the pre-baby selfishness in which most people seemed to live. Life was the best it had ever been for Julie, and it was only going to get better.

****

'Could your other half not get time off either?' Julie looked up in surprise at the woman sitting opposite her in the waiting room. They were both holding plastic cups of water, trying to fill their bladders up enough for a good result on the scan. She was much younger than Julie, not that Julie cared one bit about being an older mother anymore. She copied the empathetic smile that she had given her, tempted for a moment to blurt out the truth, the whole story, just to see her reaction, but that wasn't her style. Julie only told people what they needed to know, and so it was simpler to just go along with it.

'No, it's such a shame,' Julie said, imagining the dutiful husband at work in his office earning a fortune to keep her and their child in luxury, wishing that he could be with her for this special moment. Except that wasn't her life, but she wondered if perhaps it was the life of this stranger who wrongly presumed they had so much in common already.

'Julie Margot, room three,' the nurse called, much to Julie's relief. She stood up and walked over to put her cup in the bin. Her stomach was full of butterflies, so excited she was to see her baby. She ignored the woman's sympathy for her being here alone, Julie didn't feel lonely, or yearn for someone to be here sharing this moment with her, holding her hand. No, she needed no one apart from the little person who was growing inside her, they were all that she needed, they had each other now.

Julie knocked on the door and walked in, beaming at the nurse who sat next to the screen.

'Just hop on the bed, Julie,' she said. Julie was up on the bed in a flash. 'Now, if you can just pull your trousers down a little and your top up.'

Julie was swift in her actions, so eager to get to the point where she saw a baby on the screen.

'I'm just going to put some jelly on now, it will be a bit cold,' the nurse said, squeezing a dollop of clear gel in the middle of her stomach, and smearing it around with the ultrasound device in her hand.

Julie's eyes were glued to the screen as she looked for the shape of a baby. A round patch of darkness opened up that she presumed was her womb. As the lady concentrated on the area a grey shape started to form, the jelly baby shape she had been looking for, and her heart almost burst. Here was her *child,* someone that she could love and look after without fear they would leave her or cheat on her, or hurt her. Someone that was going to love her unconditionally, not just because she was their mother, but because she would be the best mother any child could ever wish for. This baby would have so much love, so many hugs; it would get bedtime stories and lullabies, day trips and movie nights, and she would show them the world... Julie couldn't hold back the happy tears that were coming and she turned to the nurse as she wiped them away.

'Can you tell if it's a boy or a girl, I really can't wait another twenty weeks to find out?' Julie asked. The nurse was still looking at the screen, moving the scanner around the area, pushing in a little harder. Her face was serious, and it didn't change when Julie spoke. 'Is everything okay?' she asked in a whisper. The nurse didn't answer. Julie looked back at the picture on the screen that looked just like other scan pictures she had seen; everything looked okay to her untrained eye.

'Just wait there a second, my love, I just need to get the doctor,' the nurse said, standing up. Julie didn't like the sympathy she could hear in her voice. 'Do you have anyone here with you?'

Ditched

Julie shook her head. 'No,' she said as the nurse left the room, putting her hand on her sticky stomach, 'we don't need anyone else,' she said quietly, her voice trembling.

Chapter Twenty-Two

Ditching + 41:30hrs

The camp was alive. Suddenly everyone had a story to tell, wanted to bond with their fellow survivors, was able to finally find the beauty in their surroundings now that they knew they were going to be rescued. They were elated, euphoric, and Julie tried hard to keep herself grounded, calling her crew together for what was quite possibly their final briefing.

'Right, boys and girls, it looks like we are actually going home,' she said. Her voice wobbled as she spoke, looking at these youngsters who were her responsibility, whom she needed to get back to their loved ones. She made eye contact with each of them in turn, knowing that they all had partners, parents, children who had been worrying about them since they had first ditched. It had been nearly two days since the last person had a phone signal, two days since they had been able to let anyone know that they were okay.

'It could take some time though, you all know as much as me that our rescue could be in stages, and we have no idea how quickly it will happen, so this is what I need from you...' She was thinking on her feet again. What Julie needed was a plan, direction, something to keep them focussed. 'I want us to devise a list of passengers in order of who should be rescued first. If I haven't missed anything I am going to put my poorly actor at the top of that list. I also have a hungry baby, a young girl and a diabetic lady.' She talked slowly, making sure they understood what she was asking of them. 'Now, I want you to speak to each of your passengers individually, find out if they have any medical or other reasons why they need to go first. Then we will prioritise the elderly and children, before everyone else. Is that okay?'

Her crew were all nodding in agreement.

'Fabulous,' Julie smiled. 'Now, girls, my makeup is here, you might like to reapply in case we get our photographs taken.' She passed the bag to Daisy on her left, feeling the excitement building. They were going to be rescued! Craig wasn't going to die, Reuben wouldn't starve, Bet wouldn't slip into a diabetic coma.... today was indeed a good day, she thought as she walked back to her passengers to get them excited too.

Her group were now back in their area, and Julie stopped momentarily, watching them from a distance. They had become her friends and family these last days, each one of them playing the role of people she had once imagined

213

having in her life. She smiled before starting to walk again, heading first towards Craig who was still lying on the floor with Phil kneeling by his side. As she reached them Julie's happiness subsided when she saw how pale and clammy he was, Phil looking up at her with concern written across his face despite his smile.

'How are you feeling, Craig?' Julie fixed a flight attendant smile on. She hoped that Craig didn't know how awful he looked, as she was sure his vanity would make him feel even worse than he did now, it certainly would if it were her.

'Not too bad,' Craig said, quite obviously lying.

Julie knelt down beside him, opposite to Phil. 'Brilliant, well we will have you out of here in no time and get you somewhere you can have that injury seen to properly. The rescuers are on their way.' His hair was stuck to his forehead with sweat and she swept it back with her fingers. Her mind drifted as she stroked his wavy hair back and she remembered how, not long ago, she had found him so attractive, and yet now all she saw was a young boy who needed to be cared for. She wondered if it was the fever that had changed him so much, or if it was she who had changed, if everything that had happened had altered her somehow...

'He really needs to get some antibiotics.'

Phil was talking, not to her in particular, but she nodded in response, hoping that rescue wouldn't be too long. Craig moved his head and she realised she was still stroking his hair, letting out a giggle as she pulled it away.

'I'm sorry, I was miles away, I didn't mean to keep stroking you like that,' she apologised, hoping he hadn't found her actions creepy.

'It's okay, you just reminded me of my mum, she always did that when I was a kid,' Craig said, a wistful look on his face. Julie could see that despite being all grown up, this man was wishing his mum was here right now.

'Well you can bet she will be doing it again as soon as she can get to you, she must be awfully worried right now,' Julie said kindly.

'She always worries, even though I'm a grown man.'

'Mums never stop worrying,' Julie said. It was a cliché, something she had heard so often that she felt it was okay to say, even if in her case it wasn't the truth; her mum had never worried about her, had she?

'Now you just rest up and do what the doctor says, and you will be out of here before you know it.' Julie stood up.

'Thanks, Mum,' Craig said, flashing her a cheeky smile. Julie laughed. A few days ago, she would have been horrified that a handsome young man looked at her as a motherly figure and not a sexy woman, but today it gave her a warm feeling inside, and she liked it.

She walked next to greet Ruby, who was skipping back through the tent after being outside with her mum.

'Julie, we are going home!' She threw her arms around Julie's waist and she leant down to return the hug.

'I know, sweetheart. Mummy can take you for chicken nuggets really soon, I'm so sorry you have been hungry,' she apologised.

'That's okay, it's not your fault, you've looked after us.' Ruby didn't let go as she looked up at her with her sweet face and Julie felt her eyes fill with tears for the umpteenth time. She had spent three decades 'looking after' people on board aircraft, but she had never felt so humbled doing it as she did now.

'She's right, you saved our lives, Julie, we will always be grateful to you.' Anna said, leaning forward and stroking her arm.

'No, I was just doing my job,' Julie said.

'You were, are, doing so much more than your job, don't be so British.' Anna laughed at her modesty, making Julie laugh too.

'You're my hero, Julie,' Ruby said, squeezing her.

'Wow.' Julie was overwhelmed. 'I have never been called a hero before! Thank you, Ruby, I just wish I had some of their superpowers.' Yes, she wished she could have flown them out of there, or even stopped the plane from ditching in the first place; a hero she was not, but she was very flattered that this little girl thought she was.

'Julie, I 'ave my list.' Antonio broke up the moment, and Julie let go of Ruby reluctantly.

He handed her a boarding card, on the back of which he had written the names of his passengers in order of importance for rescue.

'The first four tell me they need medication for 'art problems and diabetes,' he said, pointing out the names. 'But I don't believe 'er, the fourth one, I think she is just hungry, so I put her last.' Julie listened, trying not to laugh at Antonio's decision, presuming the lady of whom he spoke was the same one he had fallen out with at the beginning of all of this. It wasn't their place to decide who was telling the truth though, one thing that flying had taught her was that you just had to take people's word for it, believe what they told you. Like the desperate mother who tells you their baby is only ten kilos so that they can put them in a cot, when they are clearly much more, or the passenger who tells you they are allergic to something in the only meal option left, knowing you will have to find him something else. 'Then the others I have just listed in order of who is nicest...' he said. Julie opened her mouth to speak, this was perhaps a step too far ... 'I am joking, boss!' Antonio put his hand on hers to stop her, and smiled. Julie breathed out in relief. 'There are some elderly next, and then everyone under this line is young and healthy, and 'e is fit.' He pointed to one name near the bottom, nodding his head in appreciation.

Julie looked at him and wondered how she had not noticed he had a good-looking man amongst his group – usually she would have noticed them straight away.

'Well we should definitely keep him here until the end then,' she said flippantly.

'Good idea, boss.' Antonio took the list back off her and drew an arrow from the man's name to the bottom of the list. 'Let's keep all the best-looking ones here until last, it will make it much nicer.'

They were both in fits of giggles as the others came back with their lists and Antonio explained the new selection criteria. It was just harmless crew humour, the sort that not everyone understood, but it felt so good to laugh as the lists were annotated and rewritten.

'This one needs to go first, the body odour is toooo bad,' Laurence said.

'And this one can definitely stay until the end,' cooed Nadine – another handsome man Julie had missed, what was wrong with her?!

Eventually Julie broke up the party. They were getting louder, and now the lists were a mess of arrows and annotations. If the rescuers turned up imminently they would be completely disorganised.

'Right, time to focus, I'm afraid.' They giggled in silence as she explained what she thought they should do next. 'Firstly I need to collate these into one unbiased list and burn the evidence,' she said, waving the pile of boarding cards, receipts and slips of paper that she held, making them splutter as they tried to suppress their laughter. 'Meanwhile, we need to start to organise our things, get all of the equipment together, tidy up a bit...'

'Well that puts a new spin on 'Do you have to clean the plane now'?!' Jody laughed, rolling her eyes skyward. Indeed, it was a question they were asked often, and the answer was always no, but now Julie was asking them to tidy the camp and she appreciated that it sounded slightly ridiculous.

'Good point, sorry, just thinking of what we need to do,' she apologised.

'Yep, they need to write that page in the manual,' said Nadine. 'Preparing for rescue,' she said, 'Step one: Decide order of rescue based on health and *fit*ness.' The others laughed out loud now. 'Step two: Tidy Camp,' she said, putting her hand up and moving it across in the air to demonstrate the headlines.

'Okay, okay,' Julie laughed. 'Maybe just get people to gather their belongings.'

The others were becoming hysterical. 'And check their seat pockets for personal items,' added Daisy, continuing the landing PA that Julie had unwittingly quoted.

'Oh, to hell with it,' Julie laughed, exasperated, they were obviously suffering with the end-of-flight-euphoria which was common after a long day, even one as long as this. 'Do what you like, just don't do anything you might regret when it makes the papers.' She left them with the light-hearted warning, to be aware that their stories might make the news. A hero could be taken down by the press in a heartbeat, she knew that, and not for the first time that day she brushed aside the overwhelming urge to dig out the gin and get drunk on what was left. She could celebrate very soon, when she got home to her apartment and opened the bottle of Dom Pérignon that she had been saving for a special occasion... it had been there for a very long time.

Chapter Twenty-Three

12 years earlier

Julie was curled up into a ball on her sofa, the curtains pulled shut and just a sliver of light managing to break through. Today was the day that she was supposed to go to the hospital and have her baby removed, but the thought of coming back empty was unbearable. She rubbed her stomach, then patted it rhythmically, just had she had done all the way through the pregnancy… the doctors had got it wrong, she was sure of it. What if her baby was still alive and the procedure killed it? There was still a glimmer of hope, wasn't there? No, she couldn't go to the hospital, she couldn't take that risk!

She got up and walked slowly to the kitchen, feeling stiff from sleeping on the sofa and generally not moving very much. She looked at the clock; it was ten minutes to ten, she would have to leave soon if she was to make the appointment... Pouring a glass of water she gulped it down, and walked back to the lounge, sitting back in the same place, in the same pyjamas she had worn for four days now. She wasn't going anywhere.

Julie nodded in agreement with the nasty things the voices were saying. She probably would have been a terrible mum, the baby had a lucky escape. She had found herself agreeing with them about a lot these past few days, she didn't even find herself wanting them to be quiet, because then what? She would be here all alone in silence, and that would be even worse, and so she let them continue saying the same things over, and over again…

Julie closed her eyes and lay back down; she was incredibly tired, but her sleep pattern had been so erratic, two hours here and an hour there. There were some sleeping tablets in the bedroom, ones she had got from the pharmacy in Delhi, but if there was even the smallest chance that her baby was alive, she just couldn't risk harming it…

A surge of pain woke Julie up, the feeling of a band tightening around her stomach… and then it was gone. She closed her eyes again, only to be woken shortly after by another. Julie sat up, trying to relieve it, stretching one way and then the other and eventually standing. Finally it subsided again and Julie walked to the bathroom, peeling off her pyjamas and studying herself in the mirror for clues about what the pain was.

She looked thinner, and yet her stomach was still rounded, her body had been changed by the pregnancy, and whilst she would have worn stretch marks and loose skin with pride, it was a bitter pill to swallow if she would have nothing to show for it, if the doctors were right.

She looked up to her face and wondered who the person looking back at her was. An old lady stood there in her bathroom, with greasy lank hair stuck to her head. Her skin was grey and lifeless, her cheeks sunken, and deep, dark rings surrounded her sullen eyes.

Getting into the shower and setting it to cold, Julie let the water run over her body, accepting the discomfort of the coldness as some sort of penance. She was starting to side with the voices, hating herself as much as they did. The cramps came again, catching her breath with their ferocity this time, and she leaned forward, pushing her hands against the wall, counting through the pain until it went. She knew what they were now, and the thought of what was going to happen very soon made Julie go ice cold inside.

Getting out of the shower, Julie took a towel from the back of the door and wrapped it around her.

Her baby would never get to know how much love its mother had for it. Nor would she ever get to have that unconditional love she had allowed herself to dream of...

She walked into her bedroom and opened the drawer next to her bed, taking out the unopened box of sleeping tablets, sitting on the edge of her bed and popping them out one by one onto the side.

****

Julie woke up days later in a hospital bed, bewildered. It took her a while to remember everything, and when she did she lost her breath for a moment, a feeling of panic in her chest.

'You're awake, good morning, Ms Margot.'

She looked at the nurse who had appeared from nowhere and was now standing at the foot of her bed. He had big, kind eyes, and tanned skin, and was smiling at her.

'How are you feeling?' he asked, coming around to the side and sitting in the chair next to her bed.

'Okay, I guess,' Julie said. Her mouth was so dry, and he seemed to know this, handing her a glass of water which she took gratefully.

'What happened?' She didn't really want to ask, but she needed to know the rest of the story.

He leaned back in the chair before speaking. 'Well, you were found when your shower overflowed into your neighbour's downstairs and they broke in. You were very lucky.'

Julie snorted, he had no idea, and then felt immediately bad, he was only trying to be nice. So, she had left her shower running, how silly of her.

He gave her a sympathetic smile. 'It is okay, I know what you had been through, we have your medical records.

Don't be too hard on yourself, Julie.' He stood up. 'I'll let the doctor know you are awake.'

Over the next two days the kind mental-health nurse came and sat with Julie, helping her to find all of the reasons why the voices were wrong, and all the reasons she had to live. She had a great job, she had money, she was a good person... life had just dealt her a few bad cards. Besides, before she was so stupid and got pregnant, she had been doing mightily fine in life.

'Now go and live a great life, Julie,' he said as he waved her off at the hospital door.

'I will try,' she promised, sitting back in her seat and smiling. Yes, he was right, she was lucky. Julie Margot was alive and ready to have another go at living her best life, and this time she wasn't taking any chances!

Chapter Twenty-four

Ditching +42:00hrs

'Anything I can do to help?' Ken asked, making Julie sit up straight, stretching out her back. She had been sitting hunched over on this log for a fair while now, writing out every passenger and crew member's name in order of who needed rescuing first. She was so grateful for the notebook that Antonio had managed to secure from one of his group, allowing her to look organised when the rescue services finally arrived.

'Thank you, Ken, but I don't really think there is much to do until the rescuers get here, I don't want to start taking things apart in case any of us need to stay another night.' It had crossed her mind that rescue could take some time, and that she should be prepared to stay until the end. Her stomach rumbled loudly.

'Excuse me,' she apologised, embarrassed by the unladylike noise.

'Don't be daft, I think we could all do with a good meal, especially you,' he said. She looked at him, wondering what he had meant by that comment. 'Don't think I haven't noticed you have turned down your share of what food there has been at every turn.'

Julie was taken aback. It was true though, as good as the fish had smelt she hadn't taken any for herself, putting extra instead on the plates of those who needed it more. A couple of days without food certainly wouldn't do her any harm, it was harder lately to maintain her weight so a bit of fasting was not such a bad thing.

'Oh, I'm okay, I don't eat much anyway,' she reassured him. If she was honest with herself though, she was beginning to feel a little weak.

'Everyone needs to eat, Julie,' he said with a fatherly tone. 'If we have to stay tonight then I will catch you a fish all for yourself, okay?'

Julie smiled, touched by his chivalrous offer. 'That won't be necessary, but thank you.'

'We'll see,' he said, getting the last word in on the matter. 'Now, I was thinking we could start letting those flares off every half hour, you seem to have a lot of them, and make that fire smokier so that they can see it, what do you think?'

Julie raised her eyebrows. 'When did you get your wings?' she asked, amused.

'Eh?' Ken asked.

'When did you qualify as crew?' she explained, referring to his knowledge of their flares and survival training.

'I think it's the other way around, your crew seem to have military training,' he laughed. Julie paused to reflect on this. Maybe their survival training was aligned with that of the military, those few pages actually standard survival protocols? She had never thought about it any further than passing the multiple-choice questions on the exams, but she was impressed with the idea.

'Well that puts a different spin on it,' she said. 'And yes, I think that would be a fabulous idea, please keep them coming.'

Ken saluted her before walking away and she watched him for a moment, allowing herself to indulge in a bit of appreciation. She hadn't spent this long with any man for a very long time, but she knew that this one was exceptional. Strong, both physically and mentally, reliable and trustworthy, he would make somebody a wonderful partner, and she hoped he would find one, one day, who could bask in his wonderful aura. She felt a touch of sadness that she couldn't be the one, but then it was gone, replaced by the acceptance she had gained a long time ago that in order to protect herself, no one could ever get that close, and she could never give that much of herself to anyone again. The voices had crept back in a few times over these last few days, taking advantage of the situation to find her weaknesses. So far she could handle them though, and she was sure that once she got back home and away from everyone, when she could stop *caring*, they would be quiet once again.

Caring, the word took her by surprise as she thought it, it was one she hadn't thought or used for longer than she could remember. Caring was dangerous, caring left her exposed and weak. She looked over to the tent and saw Eric and Bet standing outside, and wondered if the way she felt about them, about all of them, was actually 'caring'? Ruby's little face, Reuben's smile, poor Craig... She wanted to smile as she conjured up the images, but instead her stomach flipped. She had allowed herself to see them all as part of her world, not just passengers on a plane, and in doing so she had left the lid open on her usually sealed emotional jar.

Whoosh!

A flare exploded in vivid orange smoke above them and she gazed at it as it evaporated into the air and eventually disappeared. Clearing her mind, Julie took a deep breath and looked back at the list she had just finished compiling. Soon they would all be leaving the camp and going back to their own lives, and she could get back to the one she had created for herself, where she was safe, safe from *caring*.

Chapter Twenty-five

9 years earlier

'Tits and teeth, girls, tits and teeth.' Julie pulled the trolley out of galley one and into the left-hand aisle of First Class, as another came out on the opposite side. What a treat they were in for today, a whole American football team just waiting to be served! Every seat was filled with hundreds of pounds of smooth, expensive muscle, and there was no way she was getting off this plane without securing something to make herself smile. The past three years had taught her that life was sweet, that there was so much fun to be had, as long as you protected yourself from getting hurt. So, no more relationships, not even multiple dates with the same person, a maximum of three was the limit she had set for herself. Still no close friendships, and definitely no more pregnancies... just lots of fun and living in the moment. It seemed that since she had started to live by the new and improved rules she was magnetic, and she had been living on a constant high of exciting dates and gorgeous men. She found herself showered with expensive gifts, wined and dined in the best restaurants, VIP treatment in nightclubs around the world. The girls loved flying with her because she was such great fun, and she knew that she was becoming infamous in the airline. She loved her new notoriety. Today was no exception, she wouldn't let them down.

'Would you like wine with your meal, sir?' she asked breathlessly, rubbing together her gloss-drenched lips.

'Why sure,' replied the football player. 'What you got?'

'Do you prefer red or white wine? Or perhaps champagne?' she suggested.

'Champagne would be awesome,' he said. Julie poured a glass and set it down on his table. As she leaned over she could smell his expensive aftershave.

'Celebrating?' she asked.

'Sure am,' he said, raising his glass.

'And tonight?' she asked innocently.

'Yes, miss.'

'Well perhaps us girls will see you out later, we are all heading to South Beach tonight.'

'Hey, you should join us!' His eyes lit up as he took her bait and Julie reeled in her catch.

'Really, wow, that would be amazing.' She fluttered her false eyelashes.

'Give me your number and I'll get you all on the guest list,' he said enthusiastically.

'That's so nice of you, the girls will be thrilled,' Julie gushed. 'I'll pop back with the number in a moment.'

'No problem,' he grinned, nodding his head. Julie knew that he was patting himself on the back, congratulating himself on securing him and his teammates the company of these British air hostesses this evening. Another thing she had learned was that you needed to make men believe that things were their idea in order to get what you wanted from them.

'You're a legend,' Ashleigh said quietly across the trolley as they moved along the aisle. Julie grinned; yes, she was pretty good.

'Red or white wine, sir? Or champagne?' she said with the same breathlessness to the next beautiful specimen…

Back in the galley Julie accepted her praise graciously while writing her number down for immediate delivery. 'Tonight we shall all drink champagne, girls, and dance on the tables,' she announced, waving the paper in the air and walking out. These boys were going to put them in the VIP area of a top nightclub and they were going to have so much fun, it was guaranteed like all the other times she had pulled off such feats. She put the piece of paper down on his table, making a mental note to look up his name on the manifest. That would be all she needed to know about him, she didn't need to know any more. No, she had let curiosity get the better of her once before and all it had done was make her feel bad, tainted the wonderful night out she had with that handsome CEO. After looking him up on Google, she had been forced to decline his next invitation out, through some strange misplaced loyalty to his wife and children, who she didn't even know! Now she preferred just to be ignorant; *she* was doing nothing wrong, after all.

Julie walked down the cabin, and through into Business Class, stopping to talk to a few of the passengers on her way. Her manager had contacted her just last week to tell her that she was one of his highest performing flight managers, testament to how her crew rated her, and the deluge of comments mentioning her name on the passenger surveys. She was good at her job, she was winning at life, and as long as she stuck to her own rules she would continue to do so.

'Well it was lovely to meet you, sir, if there is anything I or my crew can do for you please don't hesitate to ask,' she said, extending her hand to shake that of the suited nondescript man who had just been telling her all about his family back home and the business conference he was going to. None of it had interested Julie in the slightest, but still she had nodded and murmured in the right places, her flight attendant smile fixed throughout.

'Could I borrow a pen before you go, please? I seem to have mislaid mine,' he said, searching the inside pockets of his blazer.

'Certainly, sir.' Julie unclipped the three pens that were tucked into her waistband and held them out to him on her outstretched palm. 'Would you like Hilton, Marriott or Intercontinental? The standard pen selection off all international flight attendants, of course.'

'Thank you,' he sniggered at her joke and took the blue Hilton one.

'My pleasure,' she said politely.

Walking through the curtain into Economy she nudged open the toilet door, pleased to see that someone had recently cleaned it and that it smelt fresh. It was her pet hate recently, neglected toilets on her aircraft, so she made sure she set out her expectations as such in her pre-flight briefings. She took a step in and looked in the mirror. Her hair and makeup were still perfect, although she would need to reapply the red gloss soon, she thought…

'Defibrillator to galley four, defibrillator to galley four,' a panicked voice rang out over the PA and Julie looked at her reflection in shock.

'Shit,' she muttered under her breath as she stepped back into the aisle and walked quickly down to the galley at the back. Until now she had avoided any major situations on board, aside from the odd bit of turbulence, and she had certainly never had to get the defibrillator out. Reaching the galley, she could feel the adrenaline making her heart beat faster as she took a second to assess the situation. On the floor lay an elderly man in checked shirt and beige trousers. One of her crew was leaning over his head, blowing breaths through a resuscitation mask into his mouth, then sitting up whilst another crew member continued with chest compressions.

At the opposite door a worried-looking lady of similar age with a neat ash-blonde bob and wearing a pink twinset and pearls watched on, as a crew member stood with her arm around her shoulder in consolation.

'This is Fred, eighty-four years old, pre-existing heart condition,' Will the purser was briefing her. 'He was feeling a little breathless and generally unwell. Mary, his wife,' he looked over at the lady, 'pressed her call bell when she couldn't wake him.'

'Defib,' Julie turned to see Ashleigh wielding the piece of machinery behind her and she stepped aside to let her by.

'Thank you, Will,' Julie said. 'Carry on with CPR, you're doing a great job everyone,' she repeated the exact things that she had said during countless role plays in training. Only, this wasn't role play. It wasn't a rubber doll called Annie on the floor, it was a real man, and she could hear the cracks of his ribs as Lorraine pushed down hard and fast on his chest.

Ashleigh had already opened the defibrillator box and turned it on, while someone else had ripped open his shirt and exposed his chest in preparation.

'Apply pads,' said the mechanical voice.

'Julie, I'll call the flight deck,' said Will.

'Yes, yes, perfect,' she said. 'Ashleigh, you are doing great. Will, can you put a PA out for a doctor once you've spoken to the boys. Can *you* please phone the front and ask someone to bring down the medical kit,' she instructed the girl who was standing with Mary. For the next thirty minutes they continued relentlessly with their efforts to bring Fred back…

'No shock advised,' the mechanical voice said again. Despite rotating the crew, Julie could see that they were starting to look exhausted.

'I'm so sorry,' she said, looking at her watch and then to Mary, who was now sitting quietly crying on the jump seat. 'That's thirty minutes, you can stop now, crew. Do you agree?' She asked the question to the doctor who had come to offer his help. He had injected all sorts of drugs from the medical kit into him, but even with that, and the early defibrillation, this poor man had not been destined to reach Miami. The doctor nodded in agreement. 'Will, can you let the captain know. Time of death 1525 UTC,' she said.

****

Ditched

That night Julie drank the expensive champagne and danced on the table in VIP area of the night club, and then she went back to a party, and after that she spent the night with her chosen football player... and she thoroughly enjoyed every minute of it. Only the girls from the front galley had come out, except Ashleigh. Those that didn't were too upset, attending the debrief that the captain hosted and then choosing to go to bed and reflect on what had happened. Julie had understood as much as she could, and made sure that they were all okay, but unlike them she was absolutely fine. It wasn't that she was devoid of all feeling, of course she had been deeply sad for Fred and his poor wife, it was just that she couldn't take it personally, she had to leave it on the plane. That was how she got through life, everything belonged in its moment, not to be carried forward into the next one. Perhaps this would have worried some people, but for Julie it brought her peace from the voices, and control of her life, being so emotionally limited was a good trade as far as she was concerned.

Chapter Twenty-Six

Ditching + 44:00hrs

The whirring of the helicopter blades brought everyone out of the tent. Leaves and debris scattered around them as they shielded their eyes, all looking upward. As it hovered above them a figure emerged from the open door and began to slowly descend towards them. As he reached the ground Ken stepped forward, relieving him of the large bag he was carrying and embracing him in that masculine way that men did. Julie wasn't surprised that he seemed to know exactly what to do to help the rescuer, whereas somebody else, like her, would probably have caused a disaster if they had stepped forward so quickly. The pair of them walked towards her as the deafening noise subsided, the helicopter rising up again now that it had made its drop and flying back above the trees.

'This is Julie, she's in charge,' Ken shouted above the din to the winchman.

He was wearing goggles and a padded suit, but the huge smile on his face was one that said 'everything is okay now'. He held out his hand and took Julie's, shaking it vigorously.

'Good to meet you, Julie, we've been looking everywhere for you,' he said in a strong Canadian accent.

'We are so glad you found us,' she answered gratefully, feeling an emotional wobble in her voice. 'Here is my list of passengers and crew,' she launched straight into briefing him. 'No deaths, one injury that needs treatment soon, and the top page are people who need medication or assistance.'

'Wow, that's great.' He took the list off her and looked at it in approval. 'Pilots?'

Julie was surprised to hear the question; she had presumed they had found help by now, they had been gone for so long after all. 'No,' she shook her head, feeling concerned, 'they went off yesterday morning, two groups of three. Have you not heard from them?'

'No, ma'am, but you are miles from anywhere here, they would have struggled to find help without a map of the area.'

'So there isn't a road nearby?' Ken asked.

The winchman shook his head. 'A good few hours' walk away in these woods, and that's if you know what direction you are heading in.'

Julie felt a flash of panic as she pictured the men who had left heroically to get them help, and suddenly felt bad

239

for how she had got annoyed with Iain. He had only tried his best, and done what he thought was the right thing at the time; she had been so petty, wanting to be in charge, to show what she knew. Now he had probably been eaten by a bear, and she didn't even deserve to feel sad about it.

'Hey listen, now we have a rough idea where they've gone we can get a search party out, they'll find them, don't you worry,' he said reassuringly. Julie just nodded, hoping he was right. 'To be honest we were looking on the other side of the bay, that's where your rafts washed up.'

'We thought that was what had happened,' Ken said. 'They must have been swept away with the tide. So, what's the plan from here?'

Julie listened as they discussed the options. She wasn't in charge anymore, and she didn't want to be.

'You say you have one needing attention?'

'Yes, Craig,' Julie answered, back in the moment. 'He has a nasty infected wound and he's running a fever.'

Another one you sent out to die! Julie gulped at the truth in their venom.

'Do you think he will cope with being winched up?'

'I should say so,' Ken nodded. 'What do you think, Julie?'

'I think so, if it means he can get help sooner I think he will suffer it.'

'Good, well I'll take him with me this time, then we will need to arrange some boats. I think the best bet will be to ship you all out to Churchill,' he said thoughtfully. 'Ready for pick up, one casualty,' he said into the small microphone he wore, and a crackling voice replied. 'I will be back as soon as we have the boats arranged to lead you out, there are some supplies in the bag to distribute for now. If you can show me to the injured man.'

Julie led the way to the tent, and over to Craig, who was lying with his eyes shut.

'Craig,' she said gently, rubbing his shoulder. He opened his eyes. 'This man is going to take you to the hospital.'

'Hey, buddy,' he said, kneeling down on one knee next to him. 'Are you able to stand up and walk outside with me?'

Craig nodded weakly, accepting the help offered from Ken and Milton. Julie watched his face contort with the pain, and she felt it with him.

'Just lean on us,' Milton said, and they moved slowly outside, a grave silence all around as everyone watched on. Craig hung his head forward, and when he finally put it back up Julie could see that his eyes had rolled, that he was somewhere between awake and unconscious.

'Craig, stay with us,' she said, stepping forward and cupping his face in her hands. 'Just a few more minutes, you can do this, you hear me?' She heard the emotion in her voice as she spurred him on, fixing his eyes with hers as the helicopter appeared overhead again. This time she ignored the effect the wind had on her hair, making no attempt to hold it in place like she had earlier. She stepped aside to let the man nearer, and watched helplessly as he and Ken strapped him into the harness. The winch lowered and soon they were both rising into the sky. *Please let him be okay*, Julie thought over and over as she watched his head loll, his body seemed lifeless as it dangled in the air, before being pulled into the helicopter.

****

Julie knew she should be elated, like everyone else was; help had arrived, they all had a snack and water from the seemingly bottomless bag the nice man had left behind, and they were going to be rescued very soon, but the image of Craig's limp body just wouldn't leave her mind.

Looking for something to drown out the voices, Julie walked into the bushes to find the gin. She wouldn't have enough for anyone to notice, but she needed something. She was surprised to find Cheryl there already, nursing what was left in the bottle.

'Oh, I'm so sorry, Julie,' she apologised, her face flushed with embarrassment. 'I just had a tiny bit to take the edge off.'

'It's fine,' Julie said with a small smile, as she knew she wasn't the only one with demons to exorcise. She sat on the floor next to her and took the bottle, closing her eyes as she took the first of several sips.

'How exciting that we are getting rescued,' she said eventually, her voice not quite matching the words she had chosen. Cheryl just nodded, but she didn't say anything, her mind seemed to be somewhere else as she stared vacantly into the trees. Julie pictured the sanctuary of her apartment, the solitude that would hopefully put her back in control, that she yearned for right now as she felt her grip slipping. She fought off the images of Craig and the others, she had to hope they were all okay, or the voices would never let her forget what she did, they would never be silent again. She took another sip of the gin and passed it back to Cheryl.

'I'm going to leave him when I get back,' Cheryl said, still staring at nothing in particular, 'and this time I won't let him talk me into coming back. I'll never go back, only forward.' She said it with conviction and finally turned to look at Julie, a smile formed on her face. 'Who'd have thought it would take a plane crash and meeting you to make me finally wake up and see how shit my life was. Thank you, Julie, you saved my life twice.'

Julie was taken aback, one minute responsible for losing lives, and now being credited with saving one. *Well take that, voices*, she thought.

'I hope you find happiness, Cheryl,' Julie said sincerely.

'He won't make it easy for me, I've tried to leave before, but this time I am determined.'

'Well then you will do it. Believe me, I have been there.'

243

Cheryl looked at her in surprise. 'Now I can't believe *you* would ever have let someone treat you like *that*?'

Julie nodded. 'Yes, I did once, but that was a very long time ago.'

Cheryl had tears in her eyes. 'Well if I can come out of this half as strong a woman as you then I will think I have done well.'

Julie couldn't stop the laugh from slipping out. Strong?! 'Oh I'm not strong, Cheryl,' she said, shaking her head.

'Well I will have to disagree with you there,' Cheryl said firmly. 'How you have behaved these last days, from when we crashed to now, I think you are the strongest woman I have ever met.'

'Or I am a good actress,' Julie smirked, without further explanation. It felt nice to be having such a close conversation with someone, and she could tell that Cheryl was waiting for her to explain, to give up some details of her life's story, but this was as far as it would go, she couldn't open up any more.

'No one is that good an actress, Julie,' Cheryl said eventually, and Julie was grateful that she didn't push her for more. 'I think I speak for everyone here when I tell you that you are a strong woman.'

Julie smiled. *Did you hear that?* she asked the voices, who were still quiet. *I am a strong woman!* She waited for them to laugh, but they didn't, and the silence made her smile more. *I am a strong woman!* She repeated it over and over in her head as the gin allowed her some courage. It felt good to stand up to them, and as she repeated those few words she began to believe them.

'Here,' she said, handing the last inch of gin back to Cheryl. 'You can finish this, I guess I had better get back and start organising things.'

'I hope we will drink gin again together one day, Julie,' Cheryl said as she took the bottle.

'I would love that,' Julie said, thinking a friend would be nice. 'Somewhere that we can sit on a proper seat and not a forest floor, hey?'

Cheryl laughed as she drank some more.

I am a strong woman!

She chuckled as she emerged back into the camp, feeling infinitely more positive than she had just twenty minutes before. She stopped for a second to watch as Ruby and Anna danced under the trees on the opposite side, Anna twirling her daughter around as if there was music playing just for them. They both looked so happy, and as she stood there she was reminded of something, something so long ago it was so faint, like she had seen it on an old television. For a minute she resisted it, like she resisted all of her memories from so long ago, but something told her to let it come, to see what it was trying to show her... She could see a lady doing exactly what Anna was doing, and she could feel herself as a young girl, maybe three or four years old, twirling around like Ruby, her skirt lifting in the wind. She could feel happiness, the real, innocent happiness of a child that she hadn't remembered before. She closed her eyes to try to see better, looking at the lady, whose face was so blurred, yet so familiar... was it really her mother?

Chapter Twenty-Seven

Fifty years earlier

The music played on the record player and Vivian felt as light as a feather as she spun her daughter around in the air. The sun had broken through the clouds for the first time in months, and she could feel the darkness that had smothered her lately lifting. It wasn't that bad, just a way of life really, and she had long accepted that sadness and worry were just part of hers. But today was a good day, and she was going to enjoy every moment of it, absorb every ray of sunshine, be the mother Julie deserved, and the wife John wanted to come home to.

'Play with your toys for a little while, darling, I'm just going to fix Daddy's tea.' She leant down and patted Julie on the head, full of love for her beautiful little girl. Her daughter loved her despite everything. She forgave her for the days when she stayed in bed all day, for when she was too tired to get her lunch, or to play with her. On those days her little angel would just amuse herself and wait for the moments like this, when Mummy felt better. She forgave her when she lost her temper, and above all, she was loyal, a little confidante. She never told John what life was really like when he went to the office all day, how Mummy would stop pretending to be happy.

An hour later the front door opened and John walked in, right on time, having caught the five o'clock train home as he always did. She heard him taking off his shoes and treading lightly along the hallway towards where she was in the kitchen. Usually about now it would take some effort on her part to fix on a smile, but today it came easily.

'Good evening, darling,' she said as she stepped forward to greet him. 'I'm just cooking your favourite, chicken pie.' He looked handsome today in his navy suit, looking much younger than his thirty-five years. He always had done though, and despite the opposition from her parents she had never worried about the age gap. Still only twenty-five herself, she loved having her older man to look after her.

'We need to talk.' He didn't look at her, instead walking over to the kitchen table and sitting down, his head in his hands. Vivian stood motionless for a moment, the smile still on her face, but the happiness had been replaced by an awful sinking feeling. He didn't wait for her to join him at the table before going on. 'I can't do it anymore, I can't live with your illness, and the effect it has on our family. I want a divorce, Vivian, and I'm going to take custody of our daughter, you aren't fit for motherhood. If you get help, and get better, I will consider letting you have her at weekends.'

Vivian felt the world close in on her, the bottom fall out from beneath her, and she was falling, fast into a black hole. 'B..but..' she stuttered. 'But I've been okay, really, I've been fine lately. What have I done wrong?'

John turned to look at her. He looked tired, sad even. 'I can't worry about you anymore, Vivian. Our daughter never gets dressed, the house is never cleaned.' He moved his hand in a sweeping motion, and she saw the piles of 'stuff' that lay everywhere, that she never had the energy to sort out. On the rare good days she just wanted to play with Julie, not clean and tidy. 'You haven't been okay at all, I know that you go back to bed most days, that you just pretend. Half the time you don't take your medications... I can't do it anymore,' he said again. Now he sounded angry, resentful. So she hadn't fooled anyone, he had seen through her smiles and knew that she wasn't coping.

'I will go to the doctor, get some different tablets, set an alarm so I don't forget them,' she pleaded. It was true, she often forgot to take the antidepressants the doctor had prescribed, and even when she did take them they didn't seem to work anyway so what was the point?

'Vivian, I can't do it, I'm sorry but I've made up my mind,' he said firmly, and she burst into tears.

'But what will I do?' she asked feebly.

'I've spoken to your mother, your bedroom is ready for you. Go home, get some help.'

Vivian nodded, the tears drenching her face. 'I will, I'm so sorry that I have been such a failure,' she sobbed. When they had met she had been so fun and full of life, but since she had Julie she just hadn't been able to pull herself together. 'If I get better,' she asked in a shaky voice, 'can I come back?'

John looked at her and she knew the answer. He looked resigned, not hopeful or supportive. 'Vivian, I'm so sorry. I know you can't help it, but you have to understand how hard it has been for me.' He paused and rubbed his face with his hand. 'I've met someone else, and she is happy to care for Julie, so that you can go and get better.'

What happened after that was a blur, until Vivian woke up days later with her mother standing over her, wringing her hands in that way that had always irritated her. She thought that she looked so much older now than she remembered; although a few years had passed it seemed her mother had aged at an accelerated rate. Her hair was now completely grey and cut short, and her face had certainly lost the last of its youth, jowls forming below her hollow cheeks. As a child she had always thought her mother was so pretty, with long dark hair and bright blue eyes, but now an old lady stood here, and only the eyes had stayed the same, still as blue as the ocean and with enough worry to fill one. What age was she now, Vivian wondered, forty-five perhaps? She looked at least sixty. Was this what she had done to her own mother?

Ditched

She looked down slowly at the patchwork quilt that had lain on this, her childhood bed for as long as she could remember, and around at the cluttered shelves full of teddies and trinkets that she had collected and loved once upon a time. Now they all taunted her, mocked her for ending up back here, a failure, after she had left here so sure of herself, without a care for what it was doing to her old-fashioned parents. Now that she was a mother herself she understood a little better, and felt a twinge of guilt…

'The doctor is here to see you, love,' her mother said gently. Vivian rolled over to look at the wall. She didn't want to talk to anyone, she didn't want to think even, she just wanted to sleep and escape from everything. 'Come on, love, you want to get better and get Julie back, don't you?'

She turned back and nodded, a tear escaping. Of course she wanted to get her little girl back, although right now she felt like a little girl herself.

'Of course she does, don't you?' The same doctor who she had known all her life stepped into the room and she sat up, self-aware for the first time in days. She nodded. 'Well then let us get you the best help we can, and you'll be back to your old self in no time,' he said.

****

A few weeks later the fog began to clear as her new prescription of lithium and diazepam numbed her feelings, and Vivian felt ready to face John, desperate to see Julie. She walked up the pathway to the modest house which had been her home just two months ago and slipped her key into the lock, opening the wooden front door quietly. She didn't have a plan, she just wanted to see Julie and maybe pick up a few things, but she didn't really know what to expect. Music was playing from the sitting room, and she walked towards it, noticing how clean and tidy everything was now, and that roses from the garden had been put in a vase on the hall table. Why had she never thought to do that?

As she poked her head through the sitting room door, her heart skipped a beat when she saw Julie sitting in the middle of the floor playing with a doll which she didn't recognise, wearing a beautiful dress that she hadn't seen before. She glanced around the room, seeing the new cushions on the sofa and the way the furniture had been rearranged to make it seem so much bigger; no one else was there.

'Julie,' she whispered, putting her finger over her lips to tell her daughter to be quiet. The look in her eyes as she jumped up and ran towards her made her heart dance, just as it had that last day when they were so happy, before John had decided to tear them apart. Julie jumped into her arms and she pulled her tight towards her. As she breathed in the smell of her daughter's skin the sound of John's laughter made her look through the window into the back garden. There stood her husband with his hands on the waist of a young blonde girl with bright red lipstick, who was throwing her head back and laughing with him, swaying her hips to the music.

The anger came from nowhere as she watched them for a few brief moments, before she turned and headed for the door, carrying the only thing she needed to take from that house.

'Mummy, where are we going?' Julie asked, excited by the speed at which they ran. Finally getting onto a bus, Vivian caught her breath and sat her daughter down beside her.

'To start a new life, darling,' she smiled.

That day Vivian was full of hope, making things up as she went along. The women's shelter believed her tale about the abusive husband; after all why else would a mother and child flee with nothing like they had? They helped them to find a flat, get benefits, and to change their identity, in case the terrible man should come looking for them.

But as time went by, without her medication, and in fear of going to the doctor in case they asked too many questions, slowly she turned to alcohol as medication. Julie's memories of her father faded, and so did the ones of the happy mother, the one who loved her, danced with her, took care of her. Now her mother seesawed between sadness and anger with only the briefest glimmers of normal.

The day of Julie's tenth birthday, Vivian had a moment of clarity. It was one of those rare moments when she remembered who she really was, and felt real feelings. She wept as she realised that she hadn't even wished her daughter a happy birthday that morning, how she had been such a terrible mother. There was no way out though, she had tried and failed so many times to get better, but she couldn't do it, this was who she was now. A black cloud weighed her down with hopelessness as she took every tablet she could find. Julie would be okay, her father would come and get her and she would have a better life without her she told herself.

In the fog of despair Vivian had forgotten about the new identity, that Julie didn't even remember her real father anymore. If she had realised how her actions would impact on the one person in the world she cared about more than anything, how she would be sent into care and carry a burden of guilt her whole life, she would never have done it.

Chapter Twenty-Eight

Ditching + 47:00hrs

Julie stood in the shade of the trees and indulged in the only childhood memory she had ever had that made her feel good. It was her, and her mother, and her mother was happy. She felt loved, she could see it in her face, that she was adored. Everything that she thought she knew was changing, what she had believed about her childhood just wasn't as black and white as she had always thought; now it had colour. The bad mother that she had always remembered had once been so different. Now, the horrible drunk was a sad and pitiful person who hadn't coped with life. She wondered if she had taken her own life for the same reasons she herself had tried once, because she felt worthless, and in that moment Julie forgave her mother for everything. If anyone could understand how low you could get it was her; she just wished someone had broken in and saved her mother like they had done her, maybe with the right help she might have been okay...

'Julie, are you okay?' Jody was standing in front of her.

'Yes, my love, I am wonderful, thank you, how are you?' Julie said dreamily.

'So pleased to be getting home to my little boy, I hope they come back soon,' she said, wringing her hands, reminding Julie of her mother.

Julie reached out and brushed down a loose strand of Jody's hair that was flying away. 'They won't be long, and we will get you back to her as soon as we can. Your little boy needs his mum as much as you need him right now.'

Jody nodded. 'I can't wait.'

This warm and fluffy feeling was quite nice, Julie thought, and she let it stay for a few seconds as she watched Jody walk away, before shrugging it off in case it took hold. She might be a 'strong woman' who was actually *loved* as a child, but she was still Julie Margot, and she still had to protect herself.

'Crew brief!' she called out as she walked back into the camp, the call echoed by the ones that could hear her, until all of her crew were assembled around her in front of the now smouldering fire.

'Okaaaay,' she started. 'So just one final push, guys, until this nightmare is over!' They all looked at each other, all smiling, fidgeting with excitement. 'Now I can't promise you a pay rise, or even overtime –' everyone groaned and then giggled at her reference to the airline's reluctance to ever pay extra when they were delayed ' – but I can promise you a great night out when we finally get home, and I can tell you that each one of you has made me so proud!' Julie felt quite emotional; she didn't usually speak like this, but it just felt right. She would certainly make sure something was arranged for them all when they got back. 'We are expecting to be led down to the water to get boats to the nearest town. If you can all make sure that you have paired up anyone who might struggle with the long walk with someone fit and able, that would be great. Make sure you bring whatever you can carry easily, just in case we need anything, like the first aid kit, torches, water, flares.'

Her mind was so alert, covering all eventualities. One of the things that she had learned these past few days was that unexpected things could happen at any time! While she hoped it would be a simple walk to the shore, the sun was moving down in the sky now and it could be dark by the time they got to a boat. 'Now try and be ready so that we can get out of here as soon as the cavalry arrives. As much as I am sure you have all enjoyed your layover, I for one would like to get to a comfortable bed and a bath as soon as possible!'

'Hear hear,' said Antonio. 'If I get one more mosquito bite I will have no blood left, damn place!'

'Me too,' Laurence sympathised as they turned and walked back. Julie pondered for a moment how she actually hadn't been bitten so far, so perhaps it was true what they said about gin being a natural repellent, she mused.

Julie looked over to Milton, who was laughing with a group of the men.

'Time to let the fire go out, gentlemen,' she said sadly.

'I might just stay a few more days,' Milton said, his mouth twisted into a smile.

'Well you will have to figure out how to get out of here on your own if we are already gone,' Julie pointed out. 'I'm certainly not coming back for you,' she added as an afterthought.

'I'm sure I'll manage,' he said confidently.

'The pilots didn't, they still haven't turned up,' Julie said, immediately falling from her fluffy cloud as she remembered, her stomach sinking as she hurtled back down to earth.

'No way,' said Milton, visibly shocked by this information. 'I hope they are okay.'

'Yes, me too,' Julie said, trying to think positively. 'I am sure they will find them soon now that they know where to look. I just wish they had taken some flares.' She turned away. 'I should have told them to take flares,' she said quietly, biting her lip.

An arm came around her shoulder and she realised that it was Ken's, that he had heard her. 'It's not your fault, you can't think of everything, Julie. They will be absolutely fine, I am sure of it.'

She looked up and found some reassurance in his eyes. 'I hope so, or it will be my fault,' she said.

'No, it won't,' Ken said sternly, turning her to look at him. 'Now you have been the most amazing leader since we were still in the air, and we all owe you so much. *He* was the captain, *is* the captain,' he corrected himself, 'and he didn't need you to babysit him. He should have thought about flares himself.'

'But,' Julie began to protest.

'No,' he held a finger up, 'no buts, it is *my* birthday and I don't want to spend it arguing with you about how great you are!'

Julie had no idea what to say to that, it wasn't the first time today she had struggled to accept a compliment. 'Um, happy birthday,' she said meekly, making him laugh. 'I'm so sorry, I forgot.'

'It's okay, given the circumstances I will let you off.'

'Thank you,' she said gratefully. 'I hope we get to a hotel before the bar shuts so that we can celebrate,' she added with a grin.

'Well wouldn't that be nice, a cold glass of beer,' he said with a groan.

'Make mine a champagne,' Julie added.

'Yes, I had you down for a champagne type,' Ken said wryly. Julie couldn't help wondering if that was a good or a bad thing in his eyes, not that it mattered of course.

'I had better go and organise the rest of our group. Would you mind taking care of putting the fire out, gents? We wouldn't want the forest to burn down after we leave!'

'Yes, boss,' they all said together, making her laugh as she walked away.

Walking into the tent she headed over to where her group had all regathered. 'Hopefully it won't be long and someone will be here to get us to the water, and onto boats to a nearby town,' she briefed them.

'Wow, that'll be an adventure,' said Eric, 'won't it, Bet.'

Bet didn't seem so sure and Julie went over to see her up close. 'How are you feeling, Bet?'

'Oh I'm alright, love, just a bit tired,' she said quietly.

Julie looked at her pale skin that was starting to take on a waxy appearance. 'I think your blood sugar might be low, Bet, let me try and find you something sugary.' Julie wasn't a nurse, but this was standard medical training. She walked over to the stores area and rummaged around – nothing. Outside in the bag from the helicopter there was nothing left either, no one had thought to keep anything back since they would be getting out of there soon. She walked back to Bet and knelt down next to her. 'Bet, I need you to be honest with me. It could be a long walk back to the water, do you think you can manage it?'

'Yes, yes, I'll manage, still some strength left yet.' She smiled but Julie still wasn't convinced.

'Eric, we will get you at the front, and I'll ask Luke to help you if Bet needs extra support.' She leaned forward and rubbed Bet's arm. 'And then we will get you steak and chips for dinner.' Bet smiled.

'You're a diamond, my gal,' Eric said, suppressed emotion in his voice.

'Doing my job, Eric,' Julie smiled and moved on before anyone else could tell her she was wonderful – she might start believing them, and then she would be set for one hell of a fall.

'Luke,' she said as she approached him and Chloe. 'I was hoping you could help Eric if Bet needs some assistance when we walk back to the water. She might be a little weak as she is diabetic.'

'No problem,' he said, looking at Chloe for agreement.

'Don't worry, I can manage Reuben,' she said with a smile. 'I know exactly what you were thinking.'

Julie laughed. 'It is dangerous when someone can read your mind, Luke,' she joked. 'Thank you, though. She may not even need help but if you just walk behind them that will be great. And how are you, young man?' She looked at the grinning Reuben who was wriggling furiously to get her attention.

'I think he wants you,' Chloe laughed and held him out. Julie took him willingly and bounced him up and down. 'We were thinking, Julie,' she said and paused to look at Luke.

'We are going to get Reuben christened when we get home, and we were wondering if you would be his godmother?'

Julie froze, absolutely taken aback by the question. What did that even mean? Would she have responsibilities towards this little human, would she be expected to be part of his life? Did that mean she would actually have to care about him, not that she didn't right now, but she was fully prepared to let go of all this caring malarkey the minute she got back to her own home!

You, godmother!

Don't you think he deserves someone a bit more stable? Someone a bit better than you?

And boom, there they were! The mere thought of having to let someone in and they were ready and waiting to bring her down.

'Wow,' she said eventually, aware that everyone was watching her now, expecting her to accept the offer. 'Erm, it's such a lovely offer, but I don't think I'd be great at it, I'm not good with children generally, sorry,' she apologised and handed Reuben back to his mother awkwardly. Chloe looked crestfallen and Julie wished she could explain her problems to her. 'I'm very flattered, truly, and you know I think he's lovely, but I would hate to let him down.' She stood up, feeling terrible, and was relieved to hear the helicopter approaching.

'You'd be great, Julie, it honestly wouldn't be a responsibility, just that we would love him to grow up with you in his life, that's all. Let us know if you change your mind, it really would mean the world to us,' Chloe said. She seemed to understand, at least Julie hoped that she did.

'I promise I will think about it when we get out of here, but thank you for such a lovely offer, I'm very flattered,' she said hastily. 'Be ready to leave soon, folks,' she said loudly, heading for the door at speed.

Outside the debris was beginning to scatter again and Julie held on to her hair, realising that she had made no effort to check on her appearance. Not to worry, she thought, she would make sure her makeup bag would be included in the essential items to be taken.

Slowly another man was lowered down to them, and as last time Ken stepped out to help him.

'Military?' the man asked above the noise, and Ken shrugged.

'So where is Julie?' he asked as they walked over.

Julie was surprised to hear him ask for her by name, and put her hand up gingerly. 'Here.'

'Julie, it's a pleasure to meet you, I've been hearing about what a formidable woman you are.' He grinned and held out his hand. 'Don, very pleased to meet you, ma'am.'

Julie shook his hand but couldn't quite comprehend what he was saying; was he talking about her, and if so, who had he spoken to? 'I'm not sure where you have heard that from, but we are very happy to see you, Don.'

'From your young actor, Craig,' he explained, taking off his goggles to reveal his rugged features. 'He's gone down quite a hit at the base, and is doing very well, you will be pleased to hear.'

'Oh that is wonderful news,' Julie said, hugely relieved that he was okay. 'Any news on the others?'

'Not when I left, but I'm sure they will find them soon. They have helicopters in the air and dogs on the ground, if they are out there we'll find them.'

Julie hoped he was right.

'So, what's the plan?' Julie asked.

'Well, we have boats coming to pick you all up about a fifty-minute walk from here. Is every one fit?'

'I think so,' Julie said. 'But I have my concerns about one lady who is diabetic and seems to be hypoglycaemic.'

'I see,' he said thoughtfully. 'Well let's get everyone rounded up ready, and we will see how she is, we may need to get her lifted out if she can't make the walk.' Julie nodded, glad that there was a backup plan.

****

Slowly people began to assemble outside in groups with their assigned crew member. Julie handed out pieces of equipment to her team, giving her makeup bag to Cheryl.

'Would you mind taking that for me, Cheryl?' she said quietly, not wanting to draw attention to her frivolity.

'Of course not,' Cheryl smiled. 'As long as I can borrow some.'

'Help yourself, my dear,' Julie said. The bruise around Cheryl's eye was barely visible now, but if you knew it was there you could still see it. She hoped it would be the last bruise that Cheryl would have to cover up.

'How is the patient doing?' Phil stopped her as she walked past him. Julie wanted to ignore him, or tell him what she thought of him, but it wasn't her battle to have.

'Very well, I hear, Phil,' she said.

'Good, that's good to hear,' Phil said. 'Thank you for everything, Julie.'

Julie hadn't expected gratitude from someone like Phil, and she stopped for a moment to look at the other side to him. Perhaps his marriage was toxic but maybe deep down there was a better person inside of him, maybe something had made him the way he was.

'You are very welcome, Phil,' she said graciously.

'Right, people, listen up,' Don shouted from the front. 'You need to stay close, look out for the people around you. Any problems and we all stop. Now, is there anyone that doesn't think they can make the walk?' He paused. 'It is gonna be the best part of an hour so if you can't make it is better that you stay here and I'll send a helicopter for you.'

Julie looked around for Bet and Eric. She knew as soon as she saw them that Bet was going to struggle, but that pride and not wanting to be a burden was preventing her from saying anything. She approached Don quickly, before they started.

'Don, my lady, I don't think she will make it.'

'No problem, just get someone to wait here with her and I'll call my man back.' He was so confident, like he had saved this many people from a plane crash on multiple occasions.

'I'll stay with her,' Julie said. She felt responsible for her, and needed to know that she was okay.

'Okay, and perhaps keep your military man with you too.' He tipped his head at Ken, who had heard the conversation. Ken nodded.

'What about the husband?' Julie asked, knowing they wouldn't want to be separated.

'If he doesn't mind being airlifted, we can take two at a time, so two trips to get you all out?'

'Sounds good,' Ken agreed and Julie walked back to Eric and Bet.

'Right, you are going to stay here and they are sending a helicopter for you,' she said. 'Eric, you can stay too as long as you are happy to be airlifted, it's not for everyone.'

Julie gulped, suddenly realising that she had just volunteered herself to be winched up too; she really wasn't sure it was for her, or anyone wearing a skirt for that matter, but it was too late to back out now!

'That's fine by me, thank you,' said Eric. 'She doesn't like to be a burden, but I think it would have been too much for you too, love.' He put his arm around his wife's shoulders and led her over to a log by the fire that was now out.

Julie and Ken stood side by side as they watched everyone depart. Laurence and Antonio marched at the back, fighting playfully with their torches as light-sabres like two young boys.

'Kids,' laughed Ken, and Julie smiled as she watched them disappear into the trees, the sound of their voices slowly fading until they were left in silence except for the forest noises that had been here before they had ever arrived.

They both turned around at the same time and stood looking at the camp which lay empty now, and Julie felt inexplicably sad.

'You miss them already, don't you?' Ken said, looking at her.

Julie opened her mouth to deny it, but she couldn't, he had read her mind perfectly, she missed them.

'Don't worry, I think you've got a few friends for life there,' he said, nudging her.

'If only that were true,' she muttered.

'What is it that keeps you holding back, Julie?' Ken asked, looking at her with a frown. 'I've watched you this past two days, and wondered why such a wonderful woman won't let anyone close. Was it a bad relationship, childhood, did you get hurt?'

Nobody had ever directly asked her this before. She had always managed to run when she sensed the question was about to arise, but there was nowhere to run to, no excuse to walk away. She shrugged. 'Self-preservation,' she said simply, looking away from him.

'Against getting hurt?' Ken had a candid way of speaking to her that didn't make her feel invaded, pressured, and something about his trustworthy eyes made her want to tell him.

'Not really,' she said, thinking hard how to explain it without sounding like a complete madwoman. She pulled her cardigan around her for comfort. 'It's more what happens when I let myself get hurt, I struggle with my mental health, that's all.'

Ah that was it, the recently accepted subject of mental health. She saw it written and heard it spoken about everywhere, had done the course at work, but she had never really applied it to herself. To her, her problem was 'the voices,' and that sounded much crazier.

'Depression?' Ken asked. 'Sorry if I am asking too many questions, it's a favourite subject of mine, psychology. We are all so pressured to fit in and act normal, but everyone is wired differently.'

'I have voices,' Julie said it aloud for the first time ever, and stood stunned for a moment, hoping that she had just said it in her head. Ken didn't look shocked, perhaps she hadn't just blurted it out, perhaps he hadn't heard her; she winced.

'What do they say?' His face was still open, without judgement, and Julie inexplicably wanted to tell him more, to share her burden with him.

'That I am no good, you know, stuff like that.' She stopped short; as much as she wanted to, she couldn't bring herself to repeat everything.

'Aha,' Ken said thoughtfully. 'So, do you recognise the voices, are they anyone you know?'

Julie shook her head slowly. No, they were just voices, they didn't belong to anyone – or did they? She tried to think of what they sounded like, replaying their unkind words, a barrage of insults and put-downs, this time listening to the sounds instead of the words. Now they all sounded the same, just one voice, and something about it sounded so familiar...

'Me,' she said, looking up at Ken in shock at the realisation. He smiled back at her, as if he had worked it out before she had.

'Well maybe you should start saying nicer things, be kinder to yourself,' he said and with that he walked over to the fire and left Julie rooted to the spot, stunned.

Chapter Twenty-Nine

6 months earlier

A little bit of sunshine was just what Julie needed, as it had been raining for days in London and her mood had taken a bit of a dive. Now though she had two nights in beautiful Havana to look forward to and she was going to dance the salsa, drink mojitos, and lap up the attention of the young Cuban men who were so generous with their compliments. First though, she just had to survive this hellish flight without screaming at someone or melting into a puddle on the floor. Yes, the menopause had arrived for Julie Margot, and hit her like one big sweaty steam train. The hormone replacement therapy prescribed by the doctor would help, she was sure, but she was only two days in and was yet to feel the benefits of it.

Fanning herself with a safety card, she sat on her jump seat and opened her top button. Her brain felt like it was in a fog, she couldn't think straight, and had a strong sense that she was 'winging it', so to speak, relying on muscle memory to lead her from one stage of the flight to the next.

'We are just going to lay up, Julie,' Esther said. Julie didn't like her, her fluffy personality was so grating, but she tried to hide it, knowing that she didn't like many people right now and Esther was probably perfectly nice in another life.

'I'll just be one minute.' Julie leaned her head back and waited for the flush to subside. Why did getting older have to be so undignified, and so unattractive? Being surrounded by all of these beautiful young crew didn't help either, constantly being reminded of how you used to look but didn't anymore. She sat forward and fastened her top button again, wishing that instead of going to Havana she could just go back in time twenty years.

Hoisting herself up, she joined Esther on the cart and helped her to lay up. Her usual ease with passengers was lacking today, it was hard to make small talk when you could feel sweat trickling down your hairline. Reaching the back of the cabin, she excused herself.

'I'm going to go and help them in Economy,' she said, 'you can manage without me up here.' She smiled and darted through the curtain and straight into the sanctuary of a toilet. She didn't know if they could manage without her or not, the service might fall to pieces, but right now they were better off without her. As for going into Economy, that was a blatant lie, she definitely couldn't face the rabble down there right now!

Twenty minutes later she felt better, her temperature was no longer through the roof and a quick wash with some paper towels and soap had returned her composure somewhat. She still didn't feel right though, but if she wanted to keep flying then she had to do her job, or she would soon be pulled in for a 'chat' with her manager, whoever he was. The years of earning the right to be lazy had gone with the rise in technology, and everyone from passengers to pilots were able to pass their opinion on you these days through surveys and appraisals.

She pulled the door open and stepped into Economy, finding the crew already onto the hot drinks service. That was fine, she could do that without thinking, she thought, much less stressful than the back and forth debacle in Business. She jumped onto the end of the nearest cart and fixed on her smile.

'Coffee, tea or me, sir?' Julie asked with a big grin. She wasn't feeling particularly funny, but her work persona was well rehearsed. The young man blushed, and Julie felt a bit sorry for him, thinking perhaps she should tailor her one-liners to her audience going forward.

'No thank you,' he said, not looking at her. The girl at the other end of her cart stifled a giggle and Julie shrugged.

'Coffee tea or me,' she repeated to the next man she came to, more for her own amusement than his. He shook his head and crossed his arms like a petulant child. 'Is everything okay, sir?' Julie asked out of habit more than concern.

'Well since you ask, not really. Are you the manager?' He looked at her name badge.

'Yes, I am,' she answered politely. 'What seems to be the problem, sir?'

'Everything!' he began, having clearly been stewing for a long time and he was going to seize this opportunity to vent. Julie instantly regretted asking. 'First, I've been separated from my wife, then they ran out of everything but bloody gnocchi...' Julie tuned in and out of his moaning, she had heard it all before. Heat was beginning to rise up her neck again and she really needed to get this over with and move on before she was offering out cups of sweat. Still he moaned. 'The movie selection is rubbish. No one answered my call bell for ten whole minutes, the wine was warm...'

'Sir.' Julie had to stop him, she didn't have much time left. 'Please feel free to write in and complain.' She couldn't stand there and deal with his pettiness any longer, people in the world were having real problems right now, and her tolerance for people like *him* was at an all-time low.

'What, that's it?' His face was red for a different reason to hers. 'You call yourself a manager? No effort whatsoever to deal with any of my problems!'

Kaylie Kay

She could see he was angry now, and she knew she should calm him down and humour him, empathise, offer some means of compensation... but all she wanted to do was open a door and push him out into the clouds below them.

'Sir I just don't have time for so many complaints of so little importance,' she said, turning to the lady in the row behind who was looking at her wide-eyed. 'Coffee or tea, madam?'

'Julie, isn't it? I will be making a complaint about you,' he said with a raised voice. Everyone around was now looking at them. 'And I'm never flying with this shitty airline again!'

'Well thank heavens for that,' Julie retorted, moving the cart away from him and closer to the galley. She could feel the sweat making her shirt stick to her back, and just wanted to get this whole service over and done with so that she could take refuge once again. She stopped as they got to the toilets, where a young man stood blocking the aisle and fumbling with the door. 'Oh for goodness sake, it says PUSH so push!!' she said, shoving it open by doing exactly that. Did these people not realise she *really* needed to get out of the aisle now, that she *really* didn't have time for their complaining and dithering? She was pleased to see that at least the girl she was working with was finding the whole situation amusing as her shoulders shook with supressed laughter.

****

Ditched

The cool evening breeze felt amazing on Julie's skin as they rode around Havana in the bright pink convertible that evening. Vintage cars and horse and carts carried people between hidden gems of bars and restaurants that lay behind the untouched, bullet-holed façades that told the story of this magical place. The sound of the salsa music could be heard as they drew into the cobbled street, and the girls, already merry from drinks in the hotel, hopped over the sides of the car the minute it stopped, disappearing straight into the open-fronted bar.

The first officer, Rick, paid the driver and Julie waited for him before letting herself be swallowed up by the atmosphere that just absorbed you. A mojito soon in her hand, Julie allowed herself to be led to the dance floor by the lean, open-shirted young Cuban man who gyrated around her, taking her drink and setting it down before spinning her around and swaying his hips against hers. Julie laughed out loud, feeling so alive and happy. She knew that he would be a willing companion for the trip, shower her with compliments and attention, make her feel young again, but not this layover. No, she wasn't in control of her body right now, and until she got that control back she would be avoiding any embarrassing situations with strange men, no matter how tempted she was.

'Thank you,' she said eventually, pulling herself away, her drink calling to her. She left him on the dance floor and made her way back to her crew.

'Looks like you pulled,' Rick quipped as she sat down and picked up her drink.

'Ha ha,' Julie said. 'Just harmless fun, you should try it.' She quickly added a smile, realising that he hadn't deserved her sarcasm and wondering where it had come from. He had been nothing but sweet the whole way across. 'Sorry,' she apologised. 'Hormones.'

'Ah,' Rick laughed awkwardly and pulled a 'too much information' face that made Julie laugh back. They looked up as her dance partner swaggered towards her and Julie cringed; perhaps she was getting too old for these young men who most certainly had ulterior motives for hooking an older British lady. He beckoned her with his hands, rotating his hips and running his fingers through his shiny swept back hair. He was sweating too, about the only thing they actually had in common.

'No more,' she said, shooing him away with her hand, but he didn't seem to get the message, just coming closer, staring at her and still doing that ridiculous dance. 'No, I said,' she said with firmness.

'You know you want to,' he drawled, as if he was trying to put her under some magical spell.

'Oh for God's sake, fuck off,' Julie said, surprising herself at the sharpness of her tone. He had only been doing what she would have appreciated at any other time. 'Sorry,' she apologised again and looked at Rick to see if he had heard her uncouth comment.

'Hormones?' he looked at her in amusement.

'I can't cope,' Julie cried. 'If this HRT patch doesn't kick in soon I'm going to kill someone.' She laughed as she said it, and Rick was laughing too, making her feel instantly better.

'It's okay, I remember when my mum went through it, she was just like you,' he said kindly. 'It will get better.'

Julie appreciated the hope he was offering. 'How old is your mum now? Did it go on for long?'

'Unfortunately she died a couple of years back,' Rick said sadly.

Julie felt instantly awful. 'Oh, Rick, I'm so sorry, what happened?'

'Cancer,' he said. 'Diagnosed in the January and gone in the February.' He looked thoughtful and took a sip of his drink.

'How awful.' Julie felt suddenly emotional, full of grief for this poor man.

'Yeah, Dad took it hard, he's not been the same since.' Rick wasn't looking at her and Julie tried to wipe the tears away before anyone noticed. 'But hey, that's life.' Rick shrugged and put a smile back on his face before turning to look at her. Julie had had many such conversations about death over the years with crew, everyone had a story to tell, and it usually ended with a bit of reflection and acceptance that death was the only certainty in life. But today she couldn't cope, the tears wouldn't stop coming, and she tried hopelessly to fight the sobs that were now forcing their way out.

Rick looked at her in astonishment, before bursting into laughter again. Julie spluttered through her tears, that she just couldn't get a grip on.

'Hormones,' they both said at the same time, and laughed some more.

****

The flight home had been much better, the patch finally seemed to be working and she was remarkably dry, Julie realised as she stood by the door waiting for the engines to be switched off. A knock to the small window told her that the jet-bridge was attached and she gave a thumps up to the ground agent before standing back as they turned the handle from outside. Julie smiled as she greeted the young girl, handing her the flight paperwork first and then letting the passengers disembark.

'Goodbye, sir. Thank you, madam,' she repeated over and over, quite sure they were getting off and getting on again at the back, they were endless. *Thank heavens for Botox*, she thought as she usually did at this time, for fending off the crow's feet which would be inevitable with this much forced smiling.

Eventually they dwindled to the last few, and the crew assisted those that needed a wheelchair off the aircraft.

'Julie.' A man who she hadn't noticed before was standing at the door. He was wearing an Osprey ID and she vaguely recognised him, but she wasn't sure where from. 'I'm Andy, your manager.' He stretched his hand out and she shook it. It wasn't unusual to not know your manager, especially if like she did you tried to stay under the radar, and they seemed to change so often.

'Oh, lovely to meet you,' Julie said with more enthusiasm than she felt, hoping this wasn't going to delay her getting home. Managers only ever met the aircraft if something bad had happened, and she wondered if one of her crew had got themselves into trouble. 'How can I help you this morning?'

'I was hoping you could come back to the office with me just to discuss something, it shouldn't take too long,' he said.

'Me?' Julie asked, shocked. 'What on earth has happened?'

'Unfortunately, a passenger complained about you on the way out and we have to follow it up, I'm afraid. We just need your side of the story, that is all.'

Julie gulped; in all of her years at the airline she had never been in trouble for anything, until now. She remembered the man on the flight out, he had *actually* got off the flight and complained about her, and now she was

279

being dragged in the office for a 'chat,' one with tea and no biscuits as they were known.

'Oh, my,' Julie said. 'I am sure there has been a misunderstanding, I'll just get my things.' Her hand was shaking as she fumbled in the cupboard, changing from her flat cabin shoes into her heels and gathering her things together. All the while Andy stood with a grim look on his face at the door waiting to take her away like a court usher, and she had the distinct feeling that the verdict had already been passed, that he knew as well as she did that she was guilty.

It transpired that not only had the man complained, but his version of events had been corroborated by the lady behind. Julie cringed as Andy read out the emails, quoting what she had said, even how she had sniped at the man at the toilet door. Her only defence was her hormones, but even as she offered it in explanation she knew it in no way justified being rude to the passengers. It was her job to listen to complaints, she was the manager, and if she wasn't able to do it then she wasn't able to do the job.

Two hours later Julie got into her car and breathed deeply. She put the letter of warning into her bag; it would remind her that no matter how much she was sweating, or feeling cranky, she absolutely could not be rude to another passenger again, or at least for the next year whilst it stayed on her file. It was a pressure she could really do without given that she wasn't entirely in control of herself at the moment, but she would have to do it or she would lose her job, and what else would she do? There had never been another job for her, she had never even considered a change in career, so she really needed to be good from now on!

Chapter Thirty

Ditching + 48:00hrs

Julie stood and reflected for a while, as the camp sat silent. Now, the only sounds she could hear were the melody of the birds singing in the treetops and the murmurs of the leaves rustling in the breeze, at least she hoped it was the wind making the leaves move, and not something in the bushes. She shivered, remembering how scared she had been of the animals that lurked in the darkness when they had first arrived, until she had learned to pretend that they weren't there. She had even come to feel safe here, finding comfort in their numbers. But there were only four of them left, did that make them vulnerable now? A loud screech in the distance made her over-sensitive mind jump, and she instinctively moved closer to where Ken was. She felt immediately safer, her heart rate going back down in seconds; it was strange she thought, how he had that effect on her since they had first landed their rafts what seemed like forever ago.

Ditched

Ken was busy picking things up and making neat piles of them and Julie followed suit, thinking of the people who would be sent to clear the camp up after they had gone.

'I hope you are ready for a hero's welcome when you get home,' Ken said over his shoulder.

'Pfft, more likely my P45,' she said.

'What?' Ken stood up straight and looked at her in disbelief.

'I'm on a warning from something a few months back, I didn't bite my tongue with a passenger when I should have, so if I didn't do something right here I will be for the chop, I am sure.'

She flashed back through the last few days. Had she followed procedures? Had she missed something? Would she be in trouble again? She couldn't afford to be in trouble again, then she would be sacked, but what if someone had seen her with the gin, or she had upset someone without realising? She had been unsteady since her warning six months ago, not trusting herself, overthinking everything and checking her 'dashboard', as they called it, daily to check the scores as they came in. This job was everything she had, and if she lost it she didn't know what on earth she would do.

'I'm sure you won't be. It's quite obvious you are amazing at your job, and you've been there for years.' Ken shook his head, he clearly thought she was worrying about nothing. Julie wished he was right, and that she could take some comfort from his words, but things were different in aviation these days, she was just a number. Despite all of this, everything they had been through, she wouldn't expect any future favours in return. The computer was key, managers seemed to have lost all of their powers and discretion some years back. If she got in trouble again no one could say 'it's okay because it's you,' it just didn't work like that anymore.

'I wish you were right, but I wouldn't put it past them to send surveys to everyone about their experience, and how they rated the crew, like they do after every flight,' she said with a half-grin. Perhaps she was being a little melodramatic, but the other crew would have laughed at her cutting humour that was laced with truth. In the last couple of years it seemed the cabin crew were to blame for everything...

How did you rate your cabin crew today? Poor

Why? My seat was uncomfortable.

How did you rate your cabin crew today? Very Poor

Why? They ran out of chicken.

How would you rate your cabin crew today? Poor

Why? I didn't even fly because I was sick, and you wouldn't give me a refund.

How would you rate your cabin crew today? Poor

Why? The flight was delayed.

It was the absolute bane of their lives, but everyone had just given up fighting it.

'Well I will give you all an outstanding,' Ken said with a smile, his hands on his hips. He looked around, now that everything was neat and tidy. 'I'm going to start taking the shelter down, I'll just clear everything out of it first,' he said.

Julie followed him over, stopping to talk to Eric and Bet.

'Not long now,' she said expectantly.

'While you're here,' Eric said, taking an old phone out of his pocket and flipping it open. Julie hadn't seen a phone like that for years, and she marvelled at it for a moment. 'Let me have your number, so we can keep in touch.'

Julie hesitated; the only people she ever gave her number to were men she was interested in, not ones who wanted to stay in touch on a platonic level, this was a new one to her.

'Oh, okay it is...' She said her phone number slowly, letting Eric type it into his museum piece.

'We want you round to ours for a barbecue the first weekend we are back, meet the family,' Eric said.

'Er.' Julie wondered if she had plans in her diary, which had been lost in her handbag at the bottom of the bay, along with her phone, her clothes... she felt a tug of sadness for the first time as she thought about the things she had lost.

She knew that none of it was important of course, but they were still her things, her personal items that went with her on every trip. She would need to get a new passport too, and visas... for a moment she wished she had taken her bag off with her, but that wouldn't have looked too good she was sure, especially after she had been so bossy with Milton. Thinking about him she realised she missed her grown up scout, picturing him larking around by the fire. In fact, she missed them all, and the thought of going home and being on her own made her sadness deepen. Maybe it was time to let people be her friends in the true sense of the word?

'I won't take no for an answer,' Eric said, just as Ken came out of the tent with armfuls of blankets and emergency equipment.

'He won't,' Bet said with a smile. 'That's how he made me give in, wouldn't take no for a bloody answer.'

Eric put his arm around his wife and squeezed her. Julie looked at them, so close after all these years. There had been a brief moment in her life where she had hoped that she could have what they had, but she had long since accepted that she couldn't, and she let out an involuntary sigh.

'And bring this young fella with you,' Eric said.

'That's a very nice offer of you, I'd be happy to come,' Ken said, dropping his burden and stepping towards them. 'I'll make sure Julie comes too,' he grinned, putting his arm around her as if he had read her thought, or known what her sigh was for. She smiled as the warmth of his arm radiated into her, and she allowed herself for just a split second to enjoy it...

And then it was over, a surge of anxiety making her body stiffen, as the invisible wall shot back up around her.

Too close, too close! the voices shouted in warning. *Don't let him get too close!*

She took a step forward, releasing herself from his hold. 'I'll go and get some things out.' Julie walked quickly into the sanctuary of the empty tent, taking deep breaths to calm the panic inside of her. As it subsided she let out a snort at the ridiculousness of her reaction.

Julie walked over to where the equipment was and started to gather it up. They were right, she couldn't let him get close. *She* was right, she corrected herself. *They* didn't exist, it was just her own self-doubt and self-preservation, *she* was just looking after *herself.* She smiled as she realised that, all along she was, they were, just being her own best friend... perhaps she didn't need to be afraid of them anymore?

****

For the third time that day the sound of a helicopter made them all look to the sky. Julie held on to her hair as the wind picked up, the now familiar routine as it appeared above them and a man was slowly lowered down to the ground. With the sun setting quickly no time was wasted, and a giggling and very excited, despite her ailment, Bet was quickly strapped unceremoniously to him and winched back up. Minutes later he was back down again and Ken assisted him to strap a much less confident Eric into the harness, his face frozen in fear as they got off the ground.

'See you soon,' Julie called, waving from the side-lines. She couldn't help marvelling at how it all happened exactly as it did on television, watching the two of them suspended in mid-air, getting higher and higher until they reached the open side of the helicopter and were pulled inside by the two goggle-wearing crew onboard. It would be her turn soon, and she felt a little bit of excitement about having a new experience now that she had seen two people much older than her make it look quite easy. It used to be that new experiences happened every day for Julie, but now they were few and far between. These past few days had certainly made up for any lack of them though, she thought, that was for sure.

Julie and Ken worked largely in silence for the next hour or so, as they took down the tent and endeavoured to leave a semblance of organisation behind them, both occupied with their own thoughts. Just as the sun was starting to disappear behind the trees, the sound of the helicopter blades whirring back towards them made them both stop for the first time, and they stood side by side looking up this one last time. Julie felt an overwhelming sadness that the time here was at an end; she had learned more about herself in the time since they had ditched than she had done in her whole life before.

'So, it's a date then?' Ken asked casually, breaking her away from her reflections.

Julie turned to look at him, confused about what he meant.

'Eric and Bet's,' he reminded her, taking his eyes off the helicopter for just a moment, before looking back up at it as the winchman descended. The small smirk on his face wasn't lost on Julie, and she knew that he was teasing her.

'Well I wouldn't call it a date,' she laughed awkwardly, feeling her cheeks flush. 'But I will see you there, I am sure.'

'That's a shame,' Ken said, looking upwards still. 'I would have liked to have called it a date.'

Julie glanced sideways at him, not moving her head; the smirk was still there. She was relieved that the winchman had just reached the floor, making Ken move away. No, there would be no dates, especially with someone she actually quite liked. She had to protect herself from getting hurt, didn't she? The sadness came back, even stronger now, and she forced a smile onto her face to push the unwanted feeling back.

'Ladies first,' Ken called and Julie stepped forward eagerly. She tried to ignore the unladylike way in which the two men strapped her into the harness, tugging her skirt down at the sides in a futile attempt to preserve just a little dignity, to no avail. She clutched her shoes in her hand, waving them at Ken as he became smaller and smaller beneath them, hooting with laughter in her last burst of energy.

The exhilaration of being lifted into the helicopter was coupled with amazement as Julie gazed back down to the ground, seeing from above where they had just spent the last few extraordinary days. Ken was soon sitting by her side, and they both looked out in silence, first at their clearing and then as the helicopter travelled to their new destination, to the path they had once walked to and from the bay. The water there rippled gently with the draft of the helicopter, but nothing else around moved apart from a few birds in the sky. She tried to imagine how they must have looked to those same birds when their plane had landed there so unnaturally that day, and they had got out and casually drifted to the shore in their inflatable slide-rafts. Only the odd flash of colour from discarded life jackets evidenced the fact they had ever even been there, and in the hazy twilight even they were difficult to see now.

Still in silence, they landed in an unfamiliar small airfield, and were transferred swiftly into cars that were parked ready to receive them. Everything was laid out perfectly, and Julie was relieved that she didn't have to think about anything for the first time in so long, exhaustion overwhelming her and replacing the forced state of awareness her body had been in. They drove a short while to a hotel, on the far side of a small and unfamiliar town. In the darkness the old wooden lodge looked imposing amongst the trees, with its yellow lights filtering out through the windows. It wasn't a Marriott, that was for sure, but to Julie Margot it was the best hotel she had ever seen, her body heavy and needing to rest.

'Just to warn you, there are some local journalists here waiting,' the driver said as they pulled up at the bottom of the steps that led up to the front door. Julie looked over to the small group standing outside and groaned.

'Oh, Christ, can they not wait until I have found my makeup bag,' she complained quietly, hoping that Cheryl had been sent to the same hotel.

'Any chance we can go around the back?' Ken suggested. 'I don't think it is fair on the lady to have her photo taken now after everything she has been through.' Julie wanted to hug him for his understanding, even more so when the driver nodded and drew away quickly. Moments later they were ushered through a side door, through the kitchen, and emerged somewhat bewildered from the side of the lobby, much to the obvious surprise of the staff there.

A man of large stature in a navy suit and a name badge that said General Manager, stepped towards them. 'Ms Margot, we are honoured to have you here with us,' he said, and she felt a lump in her throat when she heard the emotion in his voice. She should have been surprised that he so instinctively knew who she was, but she was under no illusion that she looked like anything other than an airplane crash survivor right now, and she was surprisingly okay with that.

'We are pleased to be here, thank you.' Julie heard her voice tremble as she looked at the sympathetic faces all around her. It had been okay in the camp, everyone there had been in the same boat so to speak, but here they thought they were victims, that she was pitiful... it made her feel weak. She took a deep breath and pulled her shoulders back.

'If someone could just bring our luggage in,' she said, pausing before delivering the rest of her spontaneous joke. 'Oh, sorry, it's still on the plane,' she smiled and rolled her eyes, prompting them all to laugh. That was better, she was a survivor, not a victim.

'Julie.' An English voice made her turn to the side and she saw her manager standing with a serious look on his face. Her stomach lurched, and she had a terrible feeling that she was in trouble... was she about to get ditched *again?!* Had he come all this way to give her the sack from the airline?

'I know you must be exhausted, but,' he started and Julie braced herself, 'I just wanted to meet you and say that we are so proud of you at the airline. We have had so many wonderful reports about how you have looked after everyone, and I just wanted to let you know you that we will not let your efforts go unnoticed, a lot of people owe their lives to you right now.' He wore such a sincere look that she almost laughed out loud, but she managed to control herself and let him carry on uninterrupted. This was the same man standing in front of her who had asked if she thought she was up to the job just a few short months ago. At another time she might have felt contempt for him, but she was content in the knowledge that he knew as well as she did that he hadn't appreciated her back then, and so she just smiled and nodded while he carried on with his declarations of appreciation and admiration.

'We have a flight chartered for you all tomorrow evening, the details are in here.' He handed her an envelope. 'I was hoping to have a debrief with you and the pilots in the morning when you have had some sleep?'

'They are okay?' Julie's heart skipped a beat.

'Yes, yes,' her manager smiled. 'They were found a few hours ago and are tucked up in bed already.'

Julie felt awash with relief; everything really had turned out okay.

'The hotel can launder your clothes overnight, and there are robes in your rooms. Please go and get some sleep, you must be exhausted.'

Julie nodded, she was. The hotel manager led them to the lift and pressed the button for the third floor. They followed him along the corridor and Julie felt like she was on a regular trip, off to get changed to meet the crew in the bar. Aside from the fact that she had nothing to wear, she was just too tired and she turned to Ken as the door to her room opened.

'I'm so sorry we didn't get to have a drink for your birthday,' she apologised, her voice slurred now as her body prepared for sleep.

'It's okay, you can make it up to me when we get home,' he smiled. 'Besides, I've had the best birthday.'

'Okay, we will do it another day,' Julie agreed, amused that he had somehow enjoyed his birthday.

'That's a date,' he said with a tired grin, looking her straight in the eye. Julie just smiled back and walked into her room. No, it wasn't a date, but she *would* have that drink with him, after she had had one big long sleep in that huge, clean, comfortable bed which was calling out her name right now!

Chapter Thirty-One

Ditching + 58:00hrs

The water was so cold and Julie's whole body was flooded with panic. The sound of screaming was deafening as she pushed forward down the aisle, wading through as it crept up above her knees now.

'You need to get out,' she shouted, but the couple with the baby just looked hopelessly up at her from their seats, not moving, the baby just smiling at her as if she was its friend.

'Come on,' she said, tugging at the mother's arm. 'You need to get to the door, get onto the raft.' A man in a scout uniform pushed past her carrying a big case above his head, and she watched as he disappeared out of the door with it. Further down another man stood blocking the aisle getting his bag out of the overhead locker. A terrified young girl tried desperately to squeeze by him, pulling her mother by the hand, but he didn't even notice her.

'Ruby, Anna, come this way,' Julie called to them, thinking it was strange how she knew their names. But the man wouldn't move out of the way, and the water was up to Ruby's chest now. She waded forward, desperately trying to reach them.

'Madam, sir, you have to get out,' she shouted to an old couple on the other side, the water now up to their necks as they remained inexplicably sat in their seats.

'It's alright, my gal, we are okay, you get yourself out, don't worry about us,' Eric said. Yes, she knew Eric, but she just didn't know where from.

'Pleeaase, get up, Bet, you have to get out,' she pleaded, feeling tears of desperation falling down her face. They needed to get out, why were they just sitting there? Why weren't they listening to her?

'We can't swim, love,' Bet said sadly.

Julie wondered what she meant by that, she didn't need to swim. She reached the open doorway and saw that the water was halfway up it now as the plane sank further. She looked out to see countless people floating in the bay, a beautiful backdrop of tall trees lining the distant edges of the water as they bobbed around in it like bath-tub toys. Where was the raft? Why weren't they on a raft? Why didn't they all have their life jackets on too?

Julie felt her stomach flip over as she realised what she had done. She had forgotten to do the safety demo, so they hadn't known about their life jackets, and she hadn't armed her door to make sure the raft inflated! These people hadn't tried to get off because of her, because she hadn't followed her drills... she should have known better, why had she forgotten her most basic training?!

She looked in horror down the plane at the tops of people's heads. Ruby was gone, she couldn't see her, the little girl had drowned and it was all her fault. Julie stopped treading water and sank down into the abyss. She could see the sunken cabin, bodies floating around in it, but they didn't have faces. They were all calling to her though, she could hear them, telling her that it was her fault that they were dead, that she had killed them... and they were right. The water filled up her lungs and she couldn't breathe now, but it was what she deserved. Ruby's lifeless body floated past her and she tried to scream but there was no air left, she closed her eyes tightly, she couldn't stand it anymore...

'Julie.' Ken's voice was the last thing she would ever hear and she listened to it as if it were a bedtime story to fall asleep to. 'Julie, wake up,' he said. She wished that she could, but this wasn't a dream, they really had ditched... 'Julie.' Something was shaking her now and she wanted to see what it was but she was too scared to open her eyes. 'Open your eyes, you are having a bad dream,' he said with a calmness that didn't match the situation. Julie opened one eye slowly, someone was holding her and she looked up to see Ken. She shivered, realising that she was soaked with sweat and her skin was so cold underneath the robe that she had fallen asleep in. She gasped, sucking in air as if she had really been drowning and unable to breathe, her body shaking now. Ken tightened his arms and slowly the trembling subsided. Over his shoulder she saw a shadow move on the other side of the room and recognised the hotel manager. He gave her a cursory nod and let himself out.

'I heard you screaming from my room next door,' Ken explained, now cupping the back of her head in one hand. 'It was just a bad dream.' Julie nodded, letting him support her. Without words Ken moved and sat himself next to her on the bed, on top of her covers, and Julie rested her head on his chest, falling back into a deep sleep, feeling safe now that he was there to fight off her demons.

****

Julie was used to waking up in hotel rooms and wondering where she was, but this one took a lot longer to fathom. It wasn't familiar to her, and she lay still, moving only her eyes to look around. The dark wooden furniture blended into the beige walls, and the flowery bed cover just wasn't the standard chain-hotel issue that she was used to. She tried to remember what had brought her here, separating her dreams from her memories, eventually sitting up as she pieced it all together. She wondered if she had dreamt that Ken had been here in the night, because he was certainly not there now.

The dream from the night was still so vivid and she jumped up, busying herself in an effort to take her mind off it. A white envelope lay on the floor next to the door under which it had been posted, and she picked it up.

Dear Ms Margot,

Your clothes are laundered and ready for delivery, please call housekeeping when you wake.

A meeting room has been arranged for 1400, room 2312, for company debrief.

Wake up 1600

Pick up 1700

We hope you enjoyed your stay with us.

The front desk

Julie was amused at the formality of the letter, and the use of wake up and pick up times like on a normal layover, and for just a moment she wondered if she had dreamt everything. She looked at the clock; 1320 already, only forty minutes until her debrief and she needed to get ready. It wasn't lost on her that she had slept all the way through from the night before, and she felt amazing. As she stood in the shower she felt tingly with excitement, and a huge smile was spread across her face. She was excited about what the day would bring, excited to see everyone again, excited to be alive. The only thing that marred her excitement a tiny bit was when she realised she had no makeup, although she had to be grateful to the hotel for providing her with the absolute essentials, and a hairbrush.

The door knocked and Julie opened it quickly, taking the freshly laundered uniform from the porter.

'Thank you very much,' she said happily.

'You're welcome,' he smiled back. 'This was left behind the desk for you too, Ms Margot,' he said as he handed her a brown paper bag.

'Ooh,' Julie cooed, wondering what was inside. 'Thank you very much.'

The door closed behind her and she laid the clothes on the bed, opening the bag to reveal its contents. She laughed out loud when she saw her makeup bag looking back at her. 'Cheryl, you absolute star!' she said, noting that she had precisely fifteen minutes to put Julie Margot back to her best.

In the bathroom Julie opened the bag and took one last look at the Julie Margot who had been ditched. She studied her face, one that she had always covered in makeup, painted over in an effort to fool the world into believing she was who she wanted them to believe she was. But now as the real Julie looked back at her she saw who she really was for the first time... a strong woman, a survivor, a leader, and most of all someone who cared... and she really, *really* liked her. In fact, if she was to choose a best friend, she was exactly the woman she would choose!

They could have all died, she knew that, and she believed wholly that the dream had come along to make sure that she understood it. Today was the first day of the rest of her life, and only she could decide whether it was going to be full of wonderful things or whether she would carry on how she had always been, trying to protect herself from her worst enemy – herself. She shook her head at her reflection and smiled. No longer enemies, now they were going to be best friends.

For a brief moment she even considered ditching the makeup, but that thought made her laugh again at the ridiculousness of it. No, she would still wear it, but now she would wear it for different reasons, no longer to hide anything, but to emphasise what she knew about herself now, to show the world how strong she was.

Julie Margot emerged from her hotel room as immaculate as she emerged from any hotel room, but her aura was one of true confidence, of overwhelming gratitude and happiness, and she floated on her cloud to the debrief, to the car where she travelled with her pilots, and onto the plane where she was greeted with a round of applause by the passengers she had saved, and the crew who were operating this very different flight now.

The plane's captain gave an emotional briefing from the front of the plane, acknowledging how terrified they all felt, and how for reassurance this plane had just had a complete check, that this flight would go just like millions of others… without a hitch. Julie was sure that some of them would rather have walked home if they could have, but they had to believe that no one could have that much bad luck twice!

Once airborne she walked down the aircraft, making sure she spoke to every single passenger, expressing her hope that they would all meet again one day.

'I've been thinking,' she said as she took Reuben from Chloe and he giggled at her, 'I would be absolutely thrilled to be this one's godmother.'

'Julie, thank you so much, that means the absolute world to us,' Chloe gushed.

'Now I expect an invitation to the premier of your next film,' she said to Craig with a wink.

'You are my number one choice,' he said back.

'Julie, will you come and visit us?' Ruby asked sweetly.

'I would truly love that,' Julie said, stroking the little girl's hair.

'Stay in touch,' Cheryl said.

'Without a doubt,' Julie said. 'You are my gin partner,' she said in a hushed tone, their secret.

Julie looked down and noticed that Cheryl was holding Phil's hand and she was disappointed in her, until he spoke out.

'Thank you, Julie, you made me realise what I was going to lose. I'm going to get some help for my issues, I promise you both.' He looked from Cheryl to Julie, and Julie believed he meant it from the solemn look on his face. She smiled as she moved on, hoping that they would work things out, that Cheryl, like her, had found an inner strength these past days.

'Make sure you are at ours on Saturday,' Eric said. 'Meet the family.' He had a serious look on his face, telling her not to argue.

'I wouldn't miss it for all the world, Eric,' she said.

Eric and Bet smiled up at her. 'I've given our address to this fella,' Eric said pointing behind him. Julie looked behind to see Ken sitting there, waiting for her to get to him.

'It's a date,' he said, raising his eyebrow to make it a question.

'I would very much like it to be a date,' Julie said, not caring who heard, lost in the moment that was passing between her and this wonderful man who had seen her at her absolute worst and been her rock throughout everything. She could have died and never known what it was like to truly trust someone, never known what life could be like now that the voices were her friend. And she had Ken to thank for it all, him and the fate that had put him on her flight that day. She might have been applauded for saving all these lives, but *he* had saved *hers*.

The End

Acknowledgements

When I began writing Ditched I could never have imagined that by the time I finished it the world would be such a different place, that my beloved world of aviation would be in such turmoil. Like thousands of others, my wings have sadly been clipped for now. I am grateful that I managed to finish the first draft of this book on my final layover, the last time for a while that I would have the luxury of such precious alone time! I thank my airline for giving me a wonderful 22 years, and for all of the wonderful experiences that I have drawn on for my writing.

As with my other books, I couldn't have finished it without my wonderful friends, who are always so supportive of me. This time though, my biggest shout out goes to my SEP trainers, those people who drag us kicking and screaming through our yearly safety and medical training, who make sure that our knowledge of drills and procedures are branded with hot irons on our brains! It was absolutely the best thing to be able to put just a fraction of what I know into this book, to show the non-flying community how absolutely formidable us cabin crew are… passengers, you are in great hands!

If you enjoyed Ditched, I am sure that you will like my other books, The Osprey Series. Check out my website www.Kayliekaywrites.com for details of where to find them.

I love that my stories are being read by crew and aviation lovers across the globe, and it makes me so happy when I get sent photos of you reading them! You can find me on Instagram and Twitter as @kayliekaywrites, please do get in touch and send me your pictures, I would love to hear from you.

Much Love
Kaylie